Olive Logan

Apropos of Women and Theatres

With a paper or two on Parisian topics.

Olive Logan

Apropos of Women and Theatres
With a paper or two on Parisian topics.

ISBN/EAN: 9783337428594

Printed in Europe, USA, Canada, Australia, Japan

Cover: Foto ©Andreas Hilbeck / pixelio.de

More available books at **www.hansebooks.com**

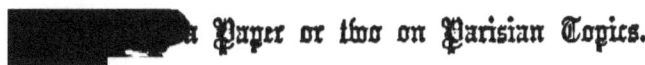PROPOS

OF

N AND THEATRES.

a Paper or two on Parisian Topics.

BY
OLIVE LOGAN.

"What I see, I say."
(After Emerson.)

NEW YORK:
CARLETON, PUBLISHER.

LONDON: S. LOW, SON, & CO.

MDCCCLXIX.

CONTENTS.

(3)

NOTE.

Some of the matter in this volume appeared originally in periodicals copyrighted according to law. Though re-written for this book, — in some cases to such a degree that little remains of the original article, — the copyrights of these periodicals are respected by the credit here given. In the following periodicals, portions of the subjoined chapters first appeared: —

Harper's Monthly Magazine,	Chapters	XII., XIII.
Putnam's Monthly Magazine,	"	XIV.
Lippincott's Magazine,	"	XV.
Packard's Monthly,	"	I., II., X.
The Galaxy,	"	VIII., IX.

THE PREFACE.

SOMETIMES I am in earnest, and sometimes I am

difficulty, my friends say, is to know when I
in earnest, — in what I write, of course.

I answer: I am in earnest when what I write is
on the side of The Right.

When I say anything that does not receive your
approval, you will at once conclude that I am in
fun.

If you run across a pun anywhere, you will of
course be animated with a Johnsonian degree of displeasure. There's the test of it. I am in fun then.

If, apropos of woman's rights, I say it is not my
nature to carp — or to fish of any kind — for faults
in the other sex: that's in fun.

If, apropos of politics, the remark being in order
that consistency is a jewel, I should say that the

1 *   (5)

consistency of most politicians is g
in fun.

If I should remark, apropos of the inter
of noisy man at woman's meetings, tha
old adage about two men he cooks spoilin
that's in fun.

But if I say anything straightforwa
and true, apropos of virtue, honor, decency,
gence, industry, and THE RIGHT, be very sure
then I am profoundly in earnest. Then I
exactly what I say, and will stand by it just
as I believe it, without much regard to anythin
the value of Truth.

OLIVE LOGAN.

AUTHORS' UNION, 264 PEARL STREET,
NEW YORK, JUNE, 1869.

APROPOS OF WOMEN AND THEATRES.

I.

ABOUT US.

Y US, I mean ourselves, of course,— women.

It is the fashion to write about Us, and it is the fashion for us to write about ourselves; but is it the fashion for other people to read what we write, or what others write about Us?

I mean, of course, on the GREAT SUBJECT,— our political, mental, moral, social, physical, and general advancement.

Anything else that is written about women, particularly if it be anything scandalous or disgraceful, is eagerly perused.

I have watched men narrowly at all sorts of

(7)

public places — in the railway car, in the omnibuses, on the boats — and I have generally observed that when there is an article in the paper about Women's Rights, men skip it quickly, and turn the newspaper inside out.

But if it is some trifling story, derogatory to the dignity of woman, or some stupid scandal about a flirtation, or some hideous relation of conjugal shame, they pore over it as if the reading of it were one of the chief duties of the day.

The fact is, that the woman question is one of those vexed ones for which it is difficult to find a satisfactory answer, which is yet hard to get around, and which is yet again apt to become prosy.

It is the negro in a white face — and petticoats.

But, if the men of our country were able to swallow the black man, I think it a wonder, indeed, if they can't get the white woman at least as far as their lips.

The mistake — or so it seems to me — of most ladies who advocate the " rights " of their sex, and also of most gentlemen who advocate the same for them, is, that their arguments are put forward in too indignant and aggressive a manner.

The result is, an indignant and aggressive reception of them by *les autres*.

I don't wonder at all (between ourselves) that these ladies are indignant and aggressive. (*Aside.*) But, dears, let's wheedle; you see we are not strong enough to knock them down, and in some respects they *are* useful, so let's gain our point by

COAXING!

Gentlemen, sweet gentlemen, amiable gentlemen, here is the woman question again.

At least, here is one woman's question:

Won't you please, like good darlings as you are, (ugh!) allow us the privilege of supporting ourselves?

Or will *you* support Us?

No, thank you, I don't mean just your own wives, and daughters, and sisters, and mothers.

I mean, will you set aside a fund for the support of the promiscuous female, so that she may not ask to vote any more, nor to enter any profession more elevated than the sewing-machinist's?

As for voting, *I* wouldn't think of doing such a thing!

No; unless I were fully satisfied my vote would be received, I would never, never wend my way to the polls.

Because, as you say, gentlemen, how unfeminine for women to meet the rough crowd — to come into contact with horrible men — who would push us and squeeze us!

It is true, we meet much the same crowd at the theatres, and in the stages and horse-cars; and, so far as my observation goes, I think women get as much squeezing in a Sixth avenue car, on a rainy afternoon, as they are likely to get at any poll that ever was raised.

With my experience of New York horse-cars, I stand prepared to meet the rude democrat, in his native shirt-sleeves, at the polls or elsewhere.

After a liberal course of horse-car, any woman who survives is qualified to vote.

It is argued that women are the inferiors, mentally, morally, and physically, of men.

Sometimes they are; and sometimes —

But I confess my weakness, when it comes to argument. In illustration lies my chief strength.

So, to illustrate:

I have a tenth cousin, who lives in Albany.

Being a man, he is mentally, morally, and physically my superior.

He has the privilege of voting, and of practising what he calls law, without invidious comment.

He has been down in New York for a week.

Literally down in New York, — down in its drinking saloons, down in its gambling Hoyles, and, finally, down in its gutters.

But, morally, he is my superior, you observe. Not merely the superior of Us, but the superior of Me.

I set him to collect a bad debt of mine two years ago. Then the man owed me two hundred dollars; now (how?) I owe him something.

That my cousin's mental faculties are more brilliant than those of poor Me is evident from this.

Finally, for two days past, he has been hanging around our office in a maudlin condition, disgracing me before my fellow-writers; and so, yesterday, when nobody was looking, I gave him a slight push, and — I haven't seen him since.

But then, physically, you know —

It seems to me if ever arguments were silly and groundless, they are those which are used to rebut the advancement of women.

Not that argument is going to prevent woman from advancing. The woman who is determined to advance *will* advance.

The trouble with most women is, that they don't get up the requisite degree of determination.

How much earnest, unflinching endeavor is any woman likely to give to any employment which, as she calculates, shall serve her purpose through two or ten years, at the end of which time she intends to get married, and throw up her occupation for ever?

Here lies the stone in the path of Us.

From our earliest years we are not taught, as boys are, that we have our fortunes in our own hands, that we must earn the bread we eat, all our lives, that we must carve out our own fortunes.

We are taught, even the poorest of Us, that marriage is our end and aim, and that as soon as we are married the man we marry will care for Us.

It is time we stopped hallooing to the world that that ugly ogre, Man, is unjust to Us.

He will marry Us, but he won't pay Us as much for our work as he will pay one of his own sex.

Alas, my sister woman! You can never earn journeymen's wages till you know your trade, and can do as good work as a man can.

You never can do that till you resolve, when you set out to learn a trade, that you will learn it thoroughly, and with the determination that at that trade you will work all the rest of your life, just as men do.

What! a woman work at her trade after marriage?

Even so. In France, this is invariably the case. Jean works no more faithfully at his occupation than does Marie at hers. She can support herself till the end of life just as easily as he can. When they marry each other, they become partners, in every sense of the word.

Their interests lie together; there is no degrading sense of dependence on the part of the wife, and marriages are happier there than with us, — divorces unknown.

I am not holding up the French people exactly as a model for imitation by our own nation; but there are some things in the French life which we can well profit by.

Let us accept a good example, though it should be set us by a nation of cannibals, — which the French are not, by the way.

Until our girls pursue their avocations as industriously and as ambitiously as our boys do, they will never become as good workers, and, consequently, they won't get as good pay.

In some of the towns out West, waiter-girls at hotel tables prevail to an alarming extent.

I say alarming, because with these girl-waiters one's best silk dress is never safe. One knows not at what moment one may have gravy bestowed upon one as a hair oil.

They are lazy, vain, pert, and inefficient to an exasperating degree.

They flirt and flit about the dining-room, lending half an ear to your demands; while both eyes, and the other ear and a half are on the watch for a husband.

Necessarily these are most unsatisfactory waiter-girls. They are, in reality, waiting girls — waiting for a husband.

It is quite impossible, under these circumstances, that girls should receive as good pay for waiting at the table as the well-drilled male waiter receives, who attends to his business, and is not on the look-out for a wife, while in the dining-room, at least.

There are certainly two branches of industry in this world where men and women stand on an absolutely equal plane in the matter of cash reward.

These are literature and the drama.

The stuff that critics write being altogether set aside, the proof of the quality of a woman's work is exactly that same matter of pay.

2*

When we bring to other avenues of labor an ambition as ardent, a zeal as earnest, as that which some of Us have brought to the theatre and the study, then will the doors open wide for Us.

Women pushed these doors open themselves, and men have given Us a seat by their side ever since, within these temples.

Mrs. Browning, Mrs. Lewes, Jean Ingelow, Madame Dudevant, Mrs. Stowe, Charlotte Brontë, Mrs. Howe, — these belong to Us.

Mrs. Siddons, Miss Cushman, Mrs. Kemble, Rachel, Ristori, Mrs. Kean, Helen Faucit, Mrs. Lander, — these belong to Us.

. And besides these, and others as distinguished in these two fields of labor, is a vast army of others, of every grade — from the poorest writer of poor poetry to the most graceful magazinist — from the littlest walking lady to the most popular star actress, — all belonging to Us.

These all receive the same reward for what they do that men on the same level receive.

The reason why is, merely that in these two departments women have long worked as men work, — with the same purpose of life-long occupation that men have. The door was long ago pushed open, and to-day stands wide.

It has long been customary for people to predict, when an actress marries off the stage, that she will speedily return to it; and to say, sneeringly, that she cannot live without the "excitement" of it.

In one case in twenty, that is true; in nineteen cases out of twenty, it is false.

An actress is a woman, who, from the moment she steps her foot on the stage to the moment she leaves it, is in receipt of a salary as good as that of an actor of the same degree.

Be that salary more or less (and it is generally more than she can earn at any other honest occupation), it is hers — her own — to spend as she likes, without question.

She marries.

Marries a young man in a dry goods store, let us say, who is manifestly making a *mesalliance* in espousing this pretty and gifted woman, whose mother is indignant at him for doing so, and

2 *

doesn't speak to him till after the first baby is born.

Thus the actress finds herself immediately in a false position; her husband feels that her position is false; and, having himself placed her in that position, at once begins to snub her for being there.

This gentleman has married on a salary of twenty dollars a week, and expects to support a family on that—when his wife has previously been in the receipt of forty a week, with no one to support but herself.

Then begin pinchings and petty questionings:

"What did you do with that dollar I gave you? Eh! Good gracious, spent fifty cents of it this morning! Well, with *your* extravagant habits, we shall soon be ruined."

And then, by and by, comes that manly cry,—

"Well, it serves me right for marrying an actress!"

Then quarrels. She has not been accustomed to rendering up an account for the merest penny in this way; she has been used to having her own money.

"Yes, but you have no money of your own now, remember that; and you must take what *I* choose to give you, or go without."

More quarrels. And, by and by, when her beauty is all gone, and she has three or four children clinging about her knees, at once augmenting and diminishing her misery, she crawls back wretchedly to the stage again.

"Ah-h-h! *I told you so.* Couldn't live without the 'excitement!' Well, he had no business to marry an actress!"

When this clerk in a dry goods store married this actress, he should have allowed her to remain on the stage.

"Oh, but that's impossible! His dignity would not allow it!"

Fudge! Emphatically, fudge! I don't believe in the dignity of a dry goods clerk.

Dry goods clerking is a woman's business, and, in passing, I would advise all young men who are now measuring tapes and ribbons to get out of it as soon as they can, and leave the occupation to that sex which is mentally, morally, and physically their inferior.

If this actress had been allowed to remain on the stage, in receipt of her forty dollars, the joint income of the couple would have been sixty dollars a week, and contentment.

How proudly, how gladly she would have turned over her earnings to her husband! How lovingly, how gratefully she would have received his tribute of praise for her labors!

That is, if she were a true and good woman. If she was not, he had no business to marry her at all, or any other such woman.

But how is a woman to attend to her household duties if she has an occupation outside of her own home?

"She must hire all her work done. If she have a large family, it will take two or three servants to attend properly to the household. Such a wasteful expense!"

If I had not heard people talk in this way, I should hardly believe it possible for human nature to be so absurd.

Do you know any man of your acquaintance —any successful business man, or any skilled workman — who would stay at home to save hiring a servant for home-work?

I have tried that kind of saving myself on several occasions, when I have had what I call the "old Ben Franklin" on me. I have sat at home in a corner for three days mending an old dress, when, if I had devoted those three days to my legitimate business — writing — I could have earned enough to buy a new dress, given the job of making it to a competent dressmaker, and the old dress to some poor woman, more needy than myself.

Now, girls, be men! Learn your business thoroughly.

Let no employer have it in his power to say your work is slovenly, and that you're only working along until you can catch *a man*; and that one man can work faster and better than three women.

If he can, of course he deserves three times your wages; but there is no good reason why you should not be as clever as he, if you will only try.

And when you are as clever as he, and can earn the wages he can, God's blessing on your union, if he asks you to be, and you consent to be, his helpmeet.

II.

ABOUT WOMAN AS A HELPMEET.

WHAT makes a woman truly a helpmeet to her husband?

In the first place, LOVE.

Without love as a first plank in the platform, there is no use whatever in discussing the question. The platform won't hold together without *that* plank, whatever other timber there be in it.

But love is not enough.

It is very sad, but it is true—and as trite as true—that "love won't boil the pot;" and what is worse, it won't put that into the pot which makes it worth the boiling.

A boiled pot wouldn't be very nice eating without "fixin's."

The beggar who made a delicious soup, just by boiling a stone in his pot, had to put in a little salt to season it, and a bit of beef to give it a flavor, and a few vegetables to tone it up.

So, if even love would "boil the pot," love would not be sufficient, unless it would fill the pot, too.

Love is the prime requisite to successful endeavor on a woman's part to be her husband's true helpmeet ; but love alone is very far from being all that is required.

There are countless thousands of women who love their husbands truly, and who are no more helpmeets to them than if they were wooden women, whittled out with a jack-knife.

I know a lady who is (in the eye of the law) married, and who does *not* love her husband. Hers is not an isolated case.

She is one of the "lucky creatures," "husband so rich," "ugly thing, how did she manage to catch him ?" etc.

She is a respectable woman, as the world goes; she hates her husband cordially, tells him and everybody so, and does not find solace, as most French women would, in a lover.

So far well. She is very severe on those poor creatures who sin in company with shame.

It is so easy, with a rich husband, to belong to that class of Christians Mrs. Browning tells us of —

> "Good Christians, who sit still in easy chairs,
> And damn the general world for standing up."

One day, not very long ago, seeing her purse full of money, one said to her, —

"How liberal your husband is to you!"

A shade of disgust passed over her face; then pointing to her three children, she said, with a shudder, —

"I earn the money he gives me."

It was a careless remark; but what a flood of truth's light poured out then!

By how much — tell me, somebody — is this woman better, in the eyes of God, who sees not as men see, than the woman who earns her money in the same way without legal ties?

Would it not be a cleaner thing, in the sight of heaven, if this woman were working, in a cotton dress, side by side with her fellow-man?

Is she, in any noble or true sense, a helpmeet to her husband?

The first and greatest misfortune women have to encounter is, that, in marrying, most men don't ask themselves whether the object of their choice is fitted to be a helpmeet. A man generally marries because he wants somebody to love him and caress him. He also wants his wife to look pretty, and be bright and cheerful, that other men may envy him his possession.

But that sort of thing won't last through the vicissitudes of a lifetime.

When years roll on, and misfortunes come, and the silly little loving wife has become firmly rooted in her dawdling habits, he savagely turns on her, and reproaches her for not being a help-meet.

There is nothing but misery for her, poor creature, after that.

Therefore, the other plank in our platform is this:

To be a true helpmeet to her husband, the woman must have the ability to earn her living independently of him.

No woman can earn her own living independently of her husband by baby-tending.

I mean, of course, by tending her own babies.
If she adopt the profession of a nurse, the case
may be different.

When you talk with intelligent MEN on the subject of skilled labor, you find that they have but
one opinion as to the best way of getting work
done thoroughly.

They tell you that the man who is a Jack-of-
all-trades is a master of none.

They tell you that the man who makes a great
success in life is the man who masters one field
of labor completely, — who educates himself up
to the highest point of skilfulness in that field
alone.

The best editors in this country are men who
have been bred to their work in that college of
editors, — the printing office.

The worst editors are those men who have
taken up editorship after having given trial to
mercantile life, or farming, or medicine, and
who will most probably drop editorship by-and-by

for the law, or perhaps the stage, and do as ill in these again, being thorough in none.

. . It stands to reason that the best baby-tender must be the woman who educates herself specially for that pursuit.

How many women who become mothers do this?

And of those women who *have* bent all their energies to perfect themselves in the art of baby-tending, how many can earn their living by it?

I once lived in a house with a young couple who had a baby of about ten months old, — a great, fine, strapping fellow, as heavy in one's arms as a load of iron, and yet unable to walk.

The father was a book-keeper in a store on Broadway, at a salary of thirty dollars a week. They paid twenty-two dollars a week for their board, which, the husband said, was as "reasonable as he could find, for a room as comfortable as the one they occupied," though I considered it far from comfortable. It was a small, back room, dull and cheerless, on the third floor.

Three times a day this delicate young girl (the baby's mother) was obliged to carry that strapping child up and down four flights of stairs to meals, —for the dining-room was in the basement. She never could get a meal in peace, for she had to hold the baby on her knees while she was eating, and it would whine and cry, and half the time she had to leave the dining-room altogether; while her great, hearty husband would sit still, and complacently bolt his meal with the utmost composure, never thinking of her.

The baby was teething; and at breakfast she often told us that she had been up and down all night long, walking the floor to soothe it.

She was as pale as a ghost, and had black rings around her eyes that were enough to startle one.

But they were so newly married, and evidently loved each other so dearly—this couple—that I thought she was as happy a woman as there was to be found in New York.

And she was a woman occupying what is facetiously denominated the "true woman's sphere;" receiving every morsel of food from her husband, every stitch of clothing, never having a penny she could call her own, and in return nursing her baby every minute from the day it was born through the successive stages of limp-backedness until now, when it seemed — except that it could not walk — stronger than its mother.

"Ah," thought I, joyfully, "here is a refutation of all my arguments. Here is a woman perfectly happy, and who is living in servitude and baby-tending!"

One day, after I had done a hard day's work at writing, I sat at the dinner table opposite the couple, and said,

"Oh, Mrs. X, how fortunate you are to have a good husband, who provides for you, and pays everything for you, relieving you of this horrid toil of working for bread-money!"

"That's what I tell her," said the husband, hastily, and with an unpleasantly triumphant tone; "if she had to go out and work for her living, she'd find out what it is."

"I *earn* my living now," said the wife, with quiet dignity; "I do a servant's work, and get no pay, — only my board. A servant gets board and wages too."

The next day she spoke to me again, with tears in her eyes, —

"I envy *you*," she said to me, who considered myself so hard worked as to be in a very unenviable position, —"I envy your being able to go out into the air, and work like an intelligent being for a livelihood, instead of being shut up, day after day, night after night, nursing a baby. I love my baby, God knows; but I do get tired nursing him sometimes. And look how foolish it is, too," continued she, unwittingly using my own arguments; "I am a fine dressmaker, and earned my living easily by that work before I was married. And so I could now, if my husband would only let me work at my trade."

"Why don't he?"

"In the first place, he is too proud; in the second, he says if I were to work I'd have to hire a girl to nurse the baby, and that would be an expense."

"How much would a girl's wages be?"

"About two dollars a week. I used to earn eighteen at dressmaking in my native town in Massachusetts. I could earn more here in New York. I'm a beautiful fitter."

And yet this couple grubbed on in mutual dissatisfaction, at the very outset of their married life, when all should have been brightness; loving each other too, but grumbling, discontented, she reproaching him for making a servant of her, and he upbraiding her for not being a helpmeet to him.

If it be necessary, in order that a woman may be a helpmeet to her husband, that she should be able to earn her own living, then she has but one thing to do to qualify herself for that office, namely, to educate herself *just as men do* in the habits of labor.

Skill in mechanism, finances, art, literature, or any industrial calling is nothing more nor less than *habits of labor.*

When men will consent to do Bridget's work, then I will.

Till then, don't talk to me about housekeeping and baby-tending as woman's only proper employment.

It is the only proper employment of women who are incapable of higher work.

The fashionable lady—the wife of a wealthy citizen—a Belmont, a Roosevelt, a Stewart, is exempt from the necessity of performing labor of any sort. She neither washes her own clothes, makes her own bed, nor devotes her time solely to the care of her babies. She has an experienced servant to do it; just as her husband has an experienced schoolmaster to teach them their lessons.

Why should not women in the humbler walks of life be granted the same immunity, so that they may be left to do more remunerative work?

Some of the religious papers have been horrified, I hear, by my views on this subject.

They are horrified, because they distort my meaning.

If any one says to me that it is necessary to NEGLECT the culture of your children's heads and hearts in order that you may be a helpmeet to your husband, I reply that such an assertion as that is rubbish.

Give me your ear, you editor, who earn the bread of your family while your wife sits at

home doing servant's work; do you neglect
your boy's mind and heart because you have
work to do out in the world?

I don't believe you do.

I don't believe, either, that it is necessary your
wife should neglect the real duties of a mother
toward her children in order to earn her share of
the yearly income which pays their nurses, their
servants, and baby-tenders.

Your wife becomes truly your helpmeet when
she can carry on your household *alone*, were you
to be taken sick or to die, as well as *you* could
were she to be taken sick or to die.

I look for the day to come when women shall
exercise freely and without reproach many privi-
leges which men now enjoy unshared, — even to
the king-privilege of the vote.

III.

 . GREAT deal has been said favorably and unfavorably in regard to granting the elective franchise to women.

I am of rather an enthusiastic nature, and my very blood boils in the kettle of my imagination, heated by the gas stove of patriotic fire, when I think of being possessor of my own poll, of having a ballot all to myself, and embroidering sweetly on the political canvass.

And then think how I could slake the thirst of my revenge on Bifkins, — Bifkins, who always steps on my dress and tears the hem, — by voting against his wife's brother, whom by the way, I never saw.

And then our next-door neighbor, Mrs. No-ton, ne'er should her husband be Mayor (if I could help it), so long as she didn't invite our Gracie to her tea-parties.

Many slights I can stand, many insults I can sit; but when it becomes a question of our Gracie's happiness, you can easily understand that my blood again boils (according to the usual custom).

What do I care whether or not Mr. No-ton is "eminently qualified for the high office"? I don't believe a word of it.

If he is, why don't his wife invite our Gracie to her tea-parties?

A very pretty girl is our Gracie. Long flaxen curls, and pinky cheeks, and teeth white as pearls.

No-ton isn't very tidy in his personal appearance, and Gracie says she thinks that any one who votes for him will-vote the dirty ticket.

But she's a little spiteful, is Gracie; and no wonder, for it was very insulting in them to invite Bifkins' girls, and leave our pretty Gracie out in the cold.

But Gracie is a brave girl, and contents herself with making faces behind No-ton's back, and assuring that wide portion of his anatomy that if

she could vote, the only office he should ever
hold would be that little dark dirty one in Pearl
street where he now belongs, and which has no
furniture in it except some nasty petroleum put
up in mysterious little bottles, looking for all the
world, each one of them, like a "dose for an adult"
of castor oil.

Gracie says she's so glad I belong to the
Pen-ian Brotherhood, because I can take mine in
hand, and have a fling at No-ton in the newspapers.

But the truth is, I am rather disgusted with the
present style of newspaper warfare; and, though I
am much offended at the No-tons' conduct, I shall
not accuse either him or his wife of highway
robbery.

That is the popular mode of expressing disapprobation now, in our chaste and elegant daily
papers.

The taste for invective seems to be growing
much more rapidly than the facility of its expression; so, thinking over the matter the other
evening, it struck me that the following exple-
tives would be rather novel and altogether
appropriate.

4

I place them quite at the disposal of whoever has occasion to use them.

For instance, we might stigmatize the different persons on the opposition ticket as—

The Wirz of the Sifth Ward.

The Black-Mailer of Beekman street.

The Caligula of modern times, now candidate for the office of Judge of the Extreme Court.

The fiddleless Nero of the Fiddlety-first district.

The Judge Jeffries of our day; now striving to get into our law courts. A hideous red tape-worm, whom nobody's vermifuge will affect.

The male Lucretia Borgia of Bond street. The sacrilegious wretch has often tried to poison the Pope's Tow with Calasaya Barque, and is even now endeavoring to throw dust in the Eyes of the Holy See.

These mild appelatives might be varied, daca-poed, accelerated, or retarded, at pleasure. Just as in a piece of music the composer gives us the motivo, and then the variations.

The motivo of using vituperative terms by these people is evident enough: one "party" doesn't want the other elected.

But did it ever strike you that if only one-nineteenth part of what the defeated party said of the other is true, why then we must be living under the rule of about as cheerful a set of scoundrels as were ever fashioned by Nature's journeymen, who didn't make them well, because they imitate Nature so abominably?

If you want me to tell you the candid, the true truth, I'll confess at once to you that the blessing of *not* being allowed to vote is one of the best-disguised blessings I ever met.

I wouldn't, on any consideration you could mention, have the responsibility of a choice in so vital a matter as choosing whether the alderman-ship should be given to McWhacker or O'Doodle.

I have a peculiar faculty for being deceived,—a stupid but unalterable belief that everybody is the best fellow in the world, which might lead me into the mistake of voting for two opposing candidates, merely because I liked them both. This little error would be awkward, wouldn't it?

It might even get me into trouble.

And then the agony of anticipating the prac-tice of that horribly iniquitous proceeding, the "gum game," which O'Doodle insists defeated Seymour; the hideous nightmare in the shape of illegal voters coming forward *en masse* and "squelching" your favorite candidate ; the lively prospect of a fight at the ballot-box, where by mistake your own party, thinking you are an opponent, pounce down upon you with clubs, and beat you lustily!

It don't help the matter much in such case when, on discovering the error, they aver that they are sorry, and intimate that a "Bourbon sour," in which they kindly will join to the number of about sixty, will set you on "your pins" again.

"Pins" indeed are your manly lower limbs as they appear in the emaciated condition after a three weeks' confinement to your room, which follows the beating you have received.

Do you stigmatize these fighters by the unmusical term "roughs"?

How slanderous! Nay, they are "gentles."

But from all these miseries,—contemplative, apprehensive and actual,—thank goodness! I am exempt. (It is so nice to have something to be thankful for!)

I'm going to add another line to my Litany :

From all voting, fighting, biting, and elections, Good Laws Deliver Us.

I am told the girls of the period are crying loudly for universal suffrage.

Wretched beings!

As if to suffer age was not already a universal complaint.

(If you should remark that this joke is venerable, I remark in reply that I can't help that. The only wonder to me is, that, considering all the witty people who have lived before us, and spoken the English language, they have left anything new under the pun still to be said.)

To be sure, there are certain situations in which excessive youth is a disadvantage.

. It would, for instance, militate against an applicant for the Premiership of England, which doubtless is the reason why the juvenescent editor of the weakly *Snarler* does not apply at once for a situation, which by his virtues and statesmanlike qualities he is so eminently fitted to hold.

Long may he wave, in the Land of the We and the Home of the Fanfaronade.

4 *

This thunder is only mine with a difference; but if the bards of other days will say all the funny things, why, *cui bono?*

(I had an idea of putting *n'importe* in there, but I remembered that French is getting rather common now, and Latin looks much more imposing, so I made it *cui bono.* It hasn't the slightest relation to the sentence, but that is altogether a minor consideration.)

Yes, as I remarked, *cui bono?* And in that case, wherefore?

The fact is, I am getting slightly mixed up here. What with age and elections, and youth and editors, my intellect totters.

I am only a woman.

I take refuge once more in the classics. What does the poet say about youth and age?

He sweetly murmurs that we gather shells from youth to age, and then we leave them like a child.

I was ever of an improvident nature, and, if you'll believe me, I haven't gathered a single shell.

If I had, I suppose I should have followed the

precept given in the same song, and flung them
one by one away, which would have put me in
the same condition as if I hadn't gathered them,
wouldn't it? Therefore—and this time I feel
my feet again on solid ground—*cui bono?*

There was a time when I might have made a
play (not a piece—Oh, no! don't mistake me) a
play on the word "shell" in relation to the elections.

There used to be "hard shells" and "soft
shells." Now I hear of these no more. The
former bearers of the name may, in a political
sense, smell as sweet by any other one, but the
word itself, the one which used to characterize
them, is apparently shellved.

So surely as the sun turns on the stick which
runs through the middle of the apple, so surely
does political, newspaperial and social slang fade
away in the west of the horizon of language, and
sink deep down into the Slough of Despond of
fleeting metaphor.

And even so sink I. When the fingers which
now clasp this valuable gold pen,—(presented me
by an admirer of literature to persuade me to

"quit"),—when those fingers, I say, have wrought their last battle, then it will be a sweet thought, that, amid all the strife and turmoil of political life, I was content to remain a woman, and never troubled my intellect about any question graver than that of the newest thing in bonnets.

IV.

I DON'T know that I altogether like the above cap-tion.

It makes me look as if I were a milliner.

But the truth is, although above all things I pride myself on being modest, I never was a modiste.

Perhaps you think it is not modest to say I am modest.

But it appears no one else will do me this justice, so what can I do but take justice in my own hands and my pen in ditto?

You know, I suppose, that the pen is mightier than the sword. This disposes of the argument that women ought to be able to bear the sword before they can be trusted with the vote.

If we can be trusted with the pen, that will do.

Few women of this generation will be called upon, let us hope, to wield the Damascene blade, or bear arms.

Sufficient to the day is the evil thereof; and while we are compelled to endure the young blade of the period, we ought not to be asked to bear any more.

By the way, how do you like "blade," as applied to the festive American youth of this century?

As our existence as a nation only stretches over a period of about ninety years, I suppose there were no American youths, festive or otherwise, of any other century; but that has nothing to do with my question.

What do you think of "blade"?

I think it is about the most nonsensical noun to apply to a man I ever heard.

It is on a par with those other charming appellatives,—"buck," and "young blood."

These are now happily obsolete.

They belong to that pedantic and conventional old school which permits, even encourages, such enormities as the words "Zounds!" and "Egad," for the use of families and schools, and has a strong penchant for "What ho!" and "Within there!" for the requirements of the restaurant.

These expressions are still in vogue on the stage, but, thank Providence, nowhere else.

In fact, a great many things are in vogue on the stage which are not the least bit so in private life.

There seems to be something in the odor of the foot-lights which chases away every atom of nature, induces a disposition to mouth words, tends to altogether destroy grace, and temporarily shows the really great disadvantage of having hands.

But I have somewhat strayed from my subject, which was — ah, yes — Bonnets.

It must be the subject is too deep for my feminine mind, or I should not continually wander away from it, and shirk it in this manner.

There is no denying that fashionable bonnets are always frightfully ugly.

The plea set up in their favor to the effect that they are "stylish" is no more founded on fact than those tales are which make the Indian a very noble creature.

But "stylish" is a fashionable word now-a-days, and is applied indiscriminately to the most extraordinary and ordinary articles.

Miss Shoddia, now *de retour* from Saratoga, has a number of stylish things; a stylish bonnet, a stylish horse, stylish gloves, a stylish coupé, and a great many very stylish beaux.

Sometimes I think she has a stylish heart as well.

It certainly is the stylish shade.

The "shade" of a heart! What an absurd expression!

Not at all. Miss Shoddia's heart is shade, not substance.

How can any woman be said to possess a heart who walks Broadway during a period of three hours every day of her life for the express, almost avowed, purpose of meeting men for whom, or for whose welfare, she does not care a button?

Indeed, buttons may be quite valuable sometimes, — as when they are set with diamonds;
but is this "style" of man, — he who walks Broadway for the purpose of meeting Shoddia, — is he
valuable?

I would not have him at any price.

If I drew him in a lottery, I should most certainly throw him back again into the box.

But what has this to do with Bonnets?

A great deal.

This is the man who, while he flatters and
cajoles poor, silly Shoddia into the belief that the
Medici Venus was the cheapest of *vin ordinaire*
compared to her lovely self, and that her costume
(not Medici's but Shoddia's) is the very perfection
of good taste and appropriateness, secretly laughs
at every separate article of which it is composed,
but particularly the bonnet.

Be its form, fashion, color, what they may, the
bonnet is quite sure to encounter ridicule at the
hands of this remorseless critic.

I never knew a bonnet to please a man yet.

It is either too large, or too small, or too gaudy,
or too plain. It is never exactly the thing,
change it often as we will.

The writers scribble against it, the carica-turists ridicule it with their pencils, the wit makes a *mot* on it, the Reverend Mr. Splurgeon de-nounces it from the pulpit.

But suppose we were to practise a little of the *lex talionis* in this vital manner. Suppose, for instance, we were to begin an indiscriminate warfare on trowsers in the abstract, or declare a state of siege against coats in the concrete. Sup-pose our animadversion extended to cravats, and we looked upon scarf-pins with the cold and pitiless eye of contempt or disgust.

Suppose, when, in the lightness of his heart and the fulness of his purse, to-day he puts forth the trembling leaves of hope, to-morrow blossoms in a pair of new boots, on the third day should come a frost, the killing frost of woman's disapproval, and then the man should fall, with the sad knowl-edge that, had he served his God with half the zeal he served his tailor, He would not, in his age, have left him naked to his enemies.

Women of America! our thraldom is too dreadful to be longer borne. We don't interfere with men's clothing: why should they torment us about ours?

I call for unanimous action in this matter; and telling action, too.

Let us rise with one accordeon, and proudly tell the monster man that, by Crinoline! we won't stand any interference.

Am I an insurrectionist?

Then so be it. If, to defend my bonnet, I must become a *sans culotte*, I am ready to accept the position, though I insist on wearing my best dress to fight in.

I am a *sans culotte en jupons*.

This being, I believe, a new idea, perhaps there is a chance of my name being handed down to posterity after all.

I hope posterity will take good care of my name, and above all not put it on the back of anybody's promissory note.

I may add, that when I shuffle off this mortal coil I am not going to advertise my death in the weakly *Snarler*.

You may call this "rambling"; in which case I shall reply, with a scornful smile, that going off to that undiscovered country, from whose bourne no traveller returns, is a pretty long ramble, as I take it.

And as you will take it some day.

After which, let us trust you will not adopt the ghost-walking "style" of the day, and come back to us in a Spiritual Photograph.

V.

I KNEW the heinous designs the man had on me; I knew that I should be called upon to endure the excruciating agony which awaits all those bleeding lambs who are mildly led to the sacrificial photographic altar. The long waiting, the fatigue of "posing," the choice of attitudes, the anxiety about back hair, the effort to look pretty, always ending in the most ignominious failure.

I knew this, and yet I went.

But the truth is, Mr. Soleil is a sophist.

A soapist is Mr. Soleil in the fullest sense of the word.

He said if I would only come to have my photograph taken, it would prove an immense advertisement for me.

5 *

He was right.

It has advertised me as being a ponderous person, stern as to eyes, and simpering as to mouth; with more nose than brains, and more cheek than either.

There are two varieties of photographic expression.

Number one, in which you endeavor to look calm and intellectual, invariably "comes out" black as a thunder-cloud in the Rain of Terror. (One great blessing attendant upon this style is that it is never recognized, even by your most intimate friends, — a circumstance which is rather trying if you happen with fatal blindness to be proud of the picture.)

Number two, in which you are requested to "sit up," to look "lively," to "smile a little," represents you trying to do all these things at once, and failing at it; but you finally succeed in distorting your features into a ghastly grin, which suggests the advisability of your immediate removal to a private Lunatic Asylum.

Mr. Soleil said if I would only come to his place, he would send a carriage for me.

I couldn't resist this appeal, and, in fact, I wanted to be free to walk Broadway again in peace without meeting the sneering smile which ever attended me when I met Soleil senior, — the sneering smile which said with Hiawathan distinctness, —

"You have broken us your promise, —
  Yes, your promise you have broken;
  You have not come to be photo'ed, —
  To be photo'ed you have not come."

Remembering this, I go.

Painfully punctual as to hour, the carriage arrives.

It is a very nice carriage, but knowing that it comes from the photographer, I experience a sense of chill and dampness on entering, which reminds me of the Tomb.

Not that I have as yet any personal knowledge of the peculiarities of the Tomb, but writers always allude to it as if they had a perfect understanding of all that takes place there, and disapproved of the "Dampness of the Tomb" on hygienic principles.

The dampness of the tomb-carriage is a secondary feature, however, as the strong smell of tobacco-smoke strikes the senses first. The lingering fragrance of the last occupant, permeating the drab cushions, fastens itself in your clothes, which must subsequently be thoroughly aired for disinfecting purposes.

This shows conclusively that air is a great thing.

The tomb-carriage moves heavily along, and at length brings up at the gallery.

Not exactly " up " at the gallery either.

It would be a great boon to stair-suffering humanity if it were so ; but what carriage can mount a half a dozen flights of stairs ? — at least in safety.

Mazeppa's may, but I am not a Mazeppa.

Why is it that photographers are always such high old fellows ?

The stairs mounted, the ordeal of undressing and re-dressing gone through with, I present myself to the " operator."

" Operator ! " Indeed a fit name. I feel exactly as if I were a dead body, and were going to be dissected.

If they would only let me act like a dead body, and be photographed lying down with my eyes shut, how grateful I should be!

But no; I must sit up or stand up. I must place myself in a graceful (?) attitude. I am requested to "throw expression" in my face, and to do all manner of things which require *exertion*, that bane of woman's existence.

I don't know how it is, I never please operators.

If I look to the right, they desire me to look to the left. If I raise my eyes to what I consider the proper height, I am peremptorily directed to lower them, and fix them on a given point, — generally a card nailed in quite a different direction to the position my body has been placed in, which circumstance has the unpleasant effect of inducing a peculiar obliquity of vision.

I do as I am bid, nevertheless, but meekly, mildly, sadly.

At one stage of the proceedings, however, I generally prove a little rebellious.

This is, when I am approached by that inquisitorial instrument of torture sarcastically denominated the "head-rest."

I long ago came to the conclusion that there is
no head-rest for the wicked who come to get
photographed.

"Must I put my head in that thing?" I ask,
eying it as if I were a conspirator, tried and condemned, and the thing in question were the
noose which was about to assist me in shuffling
off this mortal coil.

I am relieved of this necessity by the operator,
who puts it in for me, turns sundry screws, and
removes himself to a convenient distance, to
study the effect.

"Am I all right?" I ask, very tired and impatient.

The operator deigns no reply, but, taking aim
with his chemical-stained forefinger at the apex
of my nose, begins moving the former slowly
along in the regions of nowhere; while the experienced latter (which unfortunately nose all about
the photographic gesture) follows with nasalating
— I mean vacillating precision.

Ten seconds pass — ten hundred thousand
million billion seconds of agonizing quietude —

of dead-life — of non-existence — of self-eclipse (so to speak) and your photograph is taken.

Generally your life is spared.

Joyously now I prepare for departure; gleefully I release myself from the head-rest, and cease my idiotic smiling at nothing.

With a light heart, I reach the door.

There to be met by the returning operator, who, with a fiendish malignity, announces that it must *all be done over again!*

The first, which gave us both so much trouble, is a complete failure.

In the language of *nous autres*, it is knocked into photographic pi.

And it is quite evident that the chemical-stained digit, which he again raises ominously, has been a prominent finger in that pie.

But, adding affront to persecution, the operator persists that *I* spoiled the picture.

He says I "moved."

If that's all the reward I get for standing as still as a mouse is popularly supposed to, for not daring to breathe, and for staring at nothing so persistingly that it gots all blurred, and makes my eyes water, I *will* move the next time.

I'll have a physical 1st of May in full view of the camera.

I'll execute the war dance of the Catawbas, with the oscura for my vis-à-vis.

I'll do — a great many rash things. The rashest of which is to sit still again, and have my photograph done over : this time successfully.

Successfully! Heaven save the mark. I say nothing about the change in the coloring. The hair which is light coming out intensely black; the eyes which are ditto coming out — done; the complexion, that of a blonde, coming out dunnest of all.

However, thank my stars and the sun! it is over.

I don't have to pay anything, certainly, but under the circumstances I think I ought to be paid.

The sale of these photographs is immense, and is a source of handsome income to the Soleil genus.

People buy cartes-de-visite of well-known persons for as many reasons as other people resort to the convivial tumbler.

They buy them because they like us, because they dislike us, because they know us, because they don't know us, because they want to see how we look, because they want to see how we don't look, for this reason, for that reason, and for no reason whatever.

The photograph market has many fluctuations.

Let us play an engagement, successful or unsuccessful, let us write an article, clever or the reverse, let us pronounce a speech which pleases or which displeases, let us be maligned or lauded, scathed or flattered, and carte-de-visite stock goes up forthwith.

But let us be ill for a short time, unable to use our pen either cuttingly or suavely; let us get a sore throat, and be unfit for public speaking or playing; let us be obliged, in common parlance, to keep our bed, — if we have any bed to keep; let us lose step only for a few weeks in the onward march of the great army of men, and hey, presto! we drop from the ranks, and are photographically forgotten.

6

Ah! if we are only considerate enough to die, — that is a different matter! Then everybody wants a photograph.

Mr. Soleil would be in luck if he could only get hold of a "negative" of the beautiful face of the gentle genius who died yesterday in solitude and poverty. What a demand there would be for cartes-de-visite of the dead young poet!

While he lived, no photographer could have sold a hundred copies of his picture.

And thus — and thus — and thus.

Ovations to heroes, homage to greatness, the candied tongue licking absurd pomp, and crooking the pregnant hinges of the knee to what is prominent for the moment, the falsity of man, the hollowness of wealth, all fade, — and, thank God for it! they do fade, at last.

In the world to come, let us pray heaven that foremost among the joys vouchsafed us may be complete, total, entire, lasting oblivion of the mockeries of this.

In some moods, it seems to me that life is indeed all a vain and wicked show, and I could wish that the heaven of glorious angels, tuning harmonious harps, and clad in robes of light, might be a fancy of some dreamer only — the real heaven, the drab and simple paradise pictured by the Quakers.

VI.

ABOUT THE QUAKERS.

O me, the Friends are most lovable people. Their quiet presence acts like a soothing balm to my fretted spirit. Their life of unusual self-denial, their abstinence from lying, hypocrisy, sycophancy, and other hideous sins which are rife in that wicked humbug erroneously denominated the "best society," surround them with a halo of goodness and purity which I for one cannot choose but reverence.

The shad-belly coats and poke bonnets, the utter drab and decency peculiar to the sect, are visible wherever you turn in Richmond, — not the Richmond our soldiers were "on" to during the war, but Richmond in the State of Indiana. In the streets, they are on every hand; at my lecture, the audience was thickly sprinkled with them.

They yielded somewhat to the customs of the outer world while in my presence, it is true; they took off their hats when I came upon the stage; they laughed as willingly as any when the laugh came in, and wiped their eyes with their handkerchiefs in the proper places; but their costume was of orthodox simplicity.

Outsiders are apt to believe that the Quaker's dress was invented for them by some curious genius; but this is altogether a mistake. At the time George Fox appeared and founded Quakerism, the present style of Friends' dress was worn by everybody. Those were the days of Cromwell and the Commonwealth. No thought was given to the subject of dress until Cromwell's overthrow, when the Restoration brought in the piquant braveries of mincing fashion, which have gone on in unceasing change until this very hour.

It was then that the voice of this sect, which strictly denounced the vanities of the world, was lifted to anathematize, as frivolous and wicked,

6 *

these fopperies of velvet and lace, and buckle and plume. The Cromwellian costume was continued; and a strange glimpse of the past is afforded him who will but look, in thus observing men and women walking and breathing the air of to-day while wearing a style of dress which was extant in England in the era of the Protector. Use has familiarized this curious sight; but if we were to find another people wearing the dress of another age, — knee-breeches and queues, let us say, or puffs and fardengales, — how odd it would seem!

The Quaker use of "thee" and "thou" is founded on a sound principle, — that of being grammatically correct. Why the generality of us should use a plural pronoun to designate a single individual is not altogether clear. I have often had extreme difficulty in explaining this defective point to French people, who, although quite familiar with "vous" for "you," cannot comprehend the strange vagaries of a language which permits of no "thee-thouing" between lovers, parents and children, and husbands and wives.

"And then you have no thee-thou in your English?" asked a Frenchman of me one day, in the last gasp of astonishment.

"But, yes, they have," answered another, who was supposed to know English; "it is never used, however, by any bodies except the poets and the Quakkairs."

This was conclusive.

I attended "Quaker meeting" in Richmond, and was much impressed by some unusually eloquent exhortations which fell from the lips of those persons whom the spirit had moved to utter them.

These people shun the printing-press and the reporter's short-hand note-book, and thus much religious oratory of the best sort is lost to the world, while a great deal of trash is preserved for the followers of other sects to yawn over.

Discreeter use of publicity would be wise in both cases.

Ten years ago it was considered by the world at large a startling innovation on established custom for a woman to get up and address an audience.

A woman-speaker was looked upon in the most obnoxious light; she was a " Bloomerite," she was " fast," she was that terrible piece of alliteration, a " woman's-rights woman." In the extreme South, even at present, I doubt if lady-lecturers would be received with much favor.

And those persons who first went to hear women speak from the lecturer's platform of our day fancied they were assisting at something novel under the moon and stars.

Yet for two hundred plodding years before any of us were born, or, as my grandmother used loftily to say, " or thought of," women-speakers among the Friends had been lifting their voices on high, and exhorting their brethren and sisters to be good, and wise, and charitable.

When we vote, which will be soon, mind you, we must not forget to render homage where homage is due, in recognizing that the sect of Friends first practically acknowledged the equality of woman.

It was a beautiful sunny Sunday in April. The air was odorous with spring balm, and the doors and windows of the meeting-house were open wide.

In entering, the gentlemen passed in at the right, while I and my companion — a buxom Quaker lady, wife of a rich Quaker of Richmond — went in at the left.

It was a large room, with a high ceiling, bare walls, bare benches, a bare floor, with never a bare head. Every man wore his hat, every woman her bonnet.

They sat in dead silence and in rows.

Down the middle of the meeting-house, from front to back, ran a serviceable board fence, separating the hats from the bonnets.

There was no pulpit, no gallery, no organ-loft, no place at all in which to "fiddle and sing." Where the pulpit generally is were a number of slightly raised seats, on which sat row after row of the very demurest Quakers, with the very deepest bonnets, and the very broadest-brimmed hats, — men one side, women the other.

How I endured the long silence which ensued I hardly know. It was very trying to one of my disposition to sit so still.

The silence had a marked effect on me, however. There seemed to be three stages of feeling induced by it.

The first stage lasted through the first ten minutes, and was simply a feeling of blank waiting.

The second stage was comic in its character. I felt an almost irresistible impulse to create a sensation, by standing up on the bench where I sat, or by "starting the applause," with my feet, as the gallery gods do at the theatre, or some other act of desperately wicked levity.

I fell to studying the stolid faces of the elders, and an insane fancy suddenly possessed me that one of them, who sat on the top row of benches, looked like Chanfrau, the comedian.

Fancy Chanfrau with an ultra solemn face, in a Quaker hat, at a Quaker meeting!

Then another face struck me as a ludicrous imitation of that of McVicker, the Chicago manager, another comedian, and I could scarce keep from laughing outright.

The third stage quickly followed. It was one of solemn awe.

I have sat in the gorgeous and crumbling Cathedral of Notre Dame, in Paris, and listened to the impressive service of the Roman Catholic ·

Church, with its chanting priests, its wailing choir, its swinging clouds of incense; but never fell there on my soul such a religious awe as that which now took possession of me, sitting in the profound stillness of this great, barren room. I seemed to feel the presence of the Holy Ghost, with vast shadowy wings, brooding over the voiceless assemblage.

The stillness was broken by the voice of a woman, who. softly arose from her seat opposite me, and took off her ponderous bonnet.

Her face was meek and gentle, her cap was of the whiteness of snow, her hands were clasped before her.

Few of the Friends looked at her; they bent their eyes on the ground, and listened gravely. But I, with the deepest respect for her and for all, looked full at the woman-preacher.

Her dress fell in soft folds about her erect form, her 'kerchief was crossed devoutly upon her pure breast. She began in a low tone; but as she went on, her voice grew loud, and fell into a musical cadence, whose simple pathos rolled wave upon wave of tenderness across my heart.

With steadily iterating *crescendo* and *diminuendo*, like a wail, like a prayer, this woman plead to the erring to turn from their evil ways and seek the paths of peace. Her pronunciation was pure, her command of language good, her flow of ideas lucid, — all to a degree that surprised me.

Her voice died out at last in gradually falling notes, which let the overstrained feelings down to their common level, as a loving mother might lay her child gently down to sleep.

The speaker sat down, and immediately put on her bonnet.

I shall not conceal the truth, my eyes were filled with tears. All thought of the ludicrous in connection with these good people fled from me. I saw only their beautiful simplicity, calm fervor, perfect faith.

Another space of silence broken by another woman's voice, and, at the close of her remarks, a third voice — again a woman's — fell upon the serene stillness, — this time from behind me.

No head was turned to look at her.

Her voice came tremblingly, and sounded as if she were shaken like a reed, with emotion. Her syllables dropped one by one:—

"Be-lov-ed Friends,—may—these—words—sink deep into our hearts,—and bear—good fruit."

Another long silence. The sun climbed around the wall, and, as if it would lend its golden glory to this quiet scene, streamed in at the broad windows.

Presently one of the elders, a venerable man, arose and shook hands with him who sat next. Others followed the example thus set, and then the meeting was over.

The separate sexes mingled at the side door as they passed out. But, instead of trooping promptly home, as other congregations do, they gathered about the gates, the pump, the meeting-house steps, shaking hands, exchanging cheery salutations, as our grandparents did, I have read, in the olden times.

Introductions were made in the quaint Quaker style. There was no "Mr.," no "Mrs.," no "Miss."

7

"Olive!" said a sweet voice, "this is John Hardy."

"William Morehouse, this is Olive Logan."

A white-haired gentle old lady, mother of a fine-looking middle-aged gentleman who was conversing with me, was introduced as "Eliza." Everybody so addressed her,—even the little children whose grandparents had been her playmates nearly a century ago.

The whole scene was a sweet and genial one, free from cold solemnity, and will linger long in my memory.

I had pictured the Quakers in my mind as a severely sombre, solemn, sour, and altogether uncomfortable and dismal set of people.

I found them to be full of the most beautiful and winning sweetness, kind, gentle, and even affectionate toward me,—who walked a personification of that folly in attire which their religious belief unsparingly denounces.

Alas! that it should ever be so. Separated in views,—separated in creeds, in customs, in beliefs of various sorts,—we ever find, when we *meet*, as men and women, that we are not so repugnant to each other as we had perhaps imagined.

I would that those who dwell at far extremes could come together on the common plane of humanity more often. It would modify and christianize much in both which now is stern and hating.

The worthy actress, who loves virtue, honor, GOD, but whose idea of the Quaker and the puritan is drawn from the caricatures which disgrace so many otherwise excellent plays, would be astonished to find in the Quaker dame who takes her hand a gentle, true-hearted woman, worthy of her love and her respect,—not a canting Pharisee, with bitter whine and steeled heart.

The worthy Quaker lady, whose idea of all player-people is, that they serve the devil willingly, and carp at all that is pure, and good, and true, would be astonished to find that an actress may be worthy too, in spite of the vanities of the world which cling to her.

Humanity is much the same in every sphere of life, and God alone knows how closely kin may be the hearts of two women whose daily lives are as wide apart as are the Quaker meeting and the *Green-room.*

VII.

ABOUT THE GREEN-ROOM.

"YOU are fresh from Eden," said Sir Charles Pomander to the innocent young wife of Ernest Vane, when she asked the meaning of that mysterious term, the green-room. "The green-room, my dear madam, is the bower where fairies put off their wings, and goddesses become dowdies; where Lady Macbeth weeps over her lap-dog's indigestion, and Belvidera groans over the amount of her last milliner's bill. In a word, the green-room is the place where actors and actresses become mere men and women, and the name is no doubt derived from the general character of its unprofessional visitors."

This was the English green-room in the days of Peg Woffington.

An American green-room, like everything else American, has peculiarities of its own ; and Peg Woffington's *salle d'audience* differs as greatly from the green-room of Edwin Booth as the prim court of Victoria is in contrast with the profligate one of the Second Charles.

The "unprofessional visitor" is a personage almost unknown in our native green-room, and for that reason that greatest of all charms, the charm of mystery, is thrown over the hallowed precinct where the bloodthirsty Lady Macbeth becomes human enough to weep over her lap-dog's indigestion, and Belvidera pays by personal annoyance, if not in current coin, for her too reckless indulgence in milliner's wares.

That the name was derived from the habit of hanging this room with green is obvious. The reason for the selection of the color is equally obvious, and one which is still strong enough to cause its being chosen by the upholsterer for the study of his wealthy patron, green being the softest tint with which the student-eye is acquainted.

Here, then, assemble the players to study, to laugh, to chat, to put the finishing touches to

7 *

what was begun in the dressing-room, to condole with each other, to be merry, to be sad, to go through the thousand and one emotions which constitute life among players as among common folk.

The rallying-cry which brings the actors together is a small slip of paper, technically known as a "call," distributed every morning on which a rehearsal is to take place, by an humble functionary who may have a cognomen of individuality, but who is never spoken of except as the "call-boy."

He may be a call-man, but he is never so called. Like the *garçon* of the French restaurant, he retains his boyhood forever.

On this paper or "call," the hour for rehearsal, the piece to be rehearsed, and the part to be performed by the actor who receives it are all clearly written out.

Ten o'clock in the morning is the usual hour of rendezvous, and ten minutes' grace is given to allow for difference in timepieces ; any one coming later than that is subject to a fine.

A set of rules, remarkable for their stringency,

printed and framed, and hanging in grim silence in a glass case, is an inevitable ornament of every green-room.

Another ornament, and one which, besides the immense looking-glass for general use, forms the only other decoration of the walls of the green-room, is a small, square, green-lined, glass-covered box, called the " cast-case." Viewing the contents of this case, many a heart has beat high with ambitious throb, many a breast felt the bitter chill of disappointment. From it the leading tragedian learns whether he is to play Iago or Othello, Hamlet, or the shadowy murdered father of the melancholy Dane.

It tells the saucy chambermaid that she may put off cap and ribbons, and, by virtue of her singing powers, be permitted to don the conventional white muslin dress of the stage madwoman, crown her disheveled hair with wisps of straw, and play Ophelia.

But how if the leading tragedian is "cast" for some other part besides the "leading" one? What, after the arrogation of the part of Hamlet by the predatory " star " *is* the leading part in *Hamlet ?*

The manager, perhaps, leans toward the " ghost ;"
the " leading man " yearns to disport himself as
Laertes.   Here, however, the " juvenile man "
steps in, and strife begins.

But authority conquers in the green-room as
elsewhere.   The cast-case issues a fiat, against
which there is no appeal.

However, this does not prevent the uttering
of appeals, nor the making of threats of instant
departure, of leaving the theatre with the name
of the offended party in the bill for the night
(a gross contravention of stage-laws,) and other
terrors.   But the manager generally holds'firm.

At Wallack's Theatre, not long ago, the comedy of *The Wonder* was up in the cast-case, and
Mrs. Hoey was cast for Donna Violante, the leading " female " part.   The representation of the
piece was deferred, and the benefit season came
on.   Another member of the company, Miss
Fanny Morant, said she regretted not being able
to choose *The Wonder* for her benefit, as Donna
Violante, of all comedy parts, was her favorite.
In a pleasant spirit of *camaraderie*, Mrs. Hoey
offered to relinquish her right of playing this

part, allowing Miss Morant to play it for her benefit. Mr. Wallack was consulted, and agreed to
the arrangement. Some other obstacle occurred,
however, preventing the representation of the
piece for Miss Morant's benefit, and *The Wonder*
was temporarily set aside, only, after a short
lapse of time, to be replaced with the name of
Miss Henriques as Donna Violante.

Here was a blow! The leading lady could
scarcely believe her eyes. Insolent cast-case!
If it were possible to believe that the inanimate
object had of itself planned and executed this
dire affront, the lady would have believed it
rather than suspect her long-time friend, her
on-the-stage lover for ten years back, Manager
Lester Wallack, of thus deposing her. Mrs.
Hoey sought redress, but found none.

"You relinquished the part," said Mr. Wallack,
with inimitably complaisant demeanor.

"Yes," said the lady, "but only in favor of
Miss Morant, and for one occasion,—her benefit.
That part was mine by right. I am the leading
lady."

"That is indisputable," Mr. Wallack admitted

graciously. " You are the leading lady ; but you resigned the part, and, having resigned it, I am at liberty to give it to another."

In vain Mrs. Hoey's remonstrances. Mr. Wallack was firm.

" You will please accept the resignation which I now offer," said the leading lady at last, and "As you please, madam," returned the manager.

So frequent are disputes of this character that an effort is now being made to do away with the offensive cast-case altogether, by keeping the players in ignorance of the cast until each is notified of the part he is required to play through the medium of the "call."

This innovation finds no favor with actors ; for they are creatures of tradition, and such they will ever remain.

It would be useless in me to ignore, however much I might wish to do so, the social prejudice which exists against the body theatrical. How ill-grounded, how much a matter of fashion is this prejudice ; how many good and worthy people find themselves both misunderstood and unappreciated through its workings, perhaps none but one who has dwelt in the mimic world can deeply feel.

Like injustice in all its forms, this prejudice is very inconsistent; for, while the name of a poor " stock actress" is, with some people, almost a synonym for what is lax in the sex, those of Ristori and Charlotte Cushman (good and noble women in their way, and great artists without a doubt, but in point of moral worth not one whit superior to nine-tenths of other women of the theatre), are, by the same people, lauded and sung almost *ad nauseum.*

But who can account for the prejudices which are a matter of fashion?

Formerly much of the odium which now falls on the actress found its object in the milliner girls. To this day, both in London and Paris, something of this opprobrium still clings to the pretty *modiste.* Women of severe principles, governed by popular prejudice, prefer any trade to that of bonnet-making.

Absurd tyranny!

In the *School for Scandal*, it will be remembered, the lady who was hidden behind the screen in Joseph Surface's room, is described by that hypocritical moralist as a "milliner;" and the name is, of itself, sufficient to satisfy the good-natured Sir Peter that the person's character is none of the best. But, as it happens, the "petticoat" which Sir Peter "vowed he saw" was Lady Teazle herself, and thus, as not unfrequently happens, the poor milliner who was not present shouldered the fault of the fine lady who was.

It is rather extraordinary that in America, where we are supposed to have no aristocracy, the art of turning up the nose at struggling merit has reached a perfection elsewhere unknown.

While Money-Grub, of Wall Street, would feel horrified if you were to propose bringing an actor to his house, we have only to refer to the chronicles of the different periods to find that Ben Jonson was distinguished by favors from James the First, King of England and Defender of the Faith; that another actor, one Shakespeare, was not despised by a queen of the same country and its dependencies — Elizabeth.

The history of Great Britain is full of these

intimacies between court and stage. More than one coroneted head in England at the present day has worn the bauble-jewels of the "mobled queen."

Charles Mathews, travelling through Italy cheek by jowl with Lord and Lady Blessington and Count D'Orsay, could scarcely have been made to feel that his social status was much beneath that of his titled companions; for, on investigation, we find that the actor,—the merry, laughing "shoulder-slapping fellow,"—was the real lion of the party, distinguished as it was.

Sydney Lady Morgan was extremely proud of her father and mother, both players, and of their profession. She herself acted in her early youth; but, by the production of the *Wild Irish Girl*, when she gave evidence of that brilliant literary facility which entitles her to so prominent a place among English women of letters, we are led to believe that it would not be unjust to apply to her a criticism which a friend has passed on the writer of this book,—that the pen was mightier than the *comedienne*.

In France, where actresses often receive much

8

censure, and often deserve it, a distinction is still made in favor of the good. Those green-room satellites who are without reproach may also be entirely without fear.

Rose Cheri, a charming actress, whose early death all true lovers of the art must deplore, was welcome to any circle in Paris, however exclusive.

Mademoiselle Delaporte, an ingenuous young creature connected with the Gymnase Theatre, is known and respected as a worthy and amiable girl.

Mlle. Victoria, of the same theatre, received an ovation from the titled world of France on the night of her reappearance after her marriage with an actor of the company.

Belonging, root and branch, to a theatrical family, — born, figuratively speaking, in the green-room, I have not on that account been deemed unworthy to break bread at an imperial table, nor to take the hand of friendship extended by an English lordly divine.

My reader may perhaps feel like reminding me of certain celebrated players of great wealth

and national fame, who have not felt social os-
tracism in this country, and that their reception
by the *beau monde* is a partial refutation of my
strictures.

I scarcely recognize that this is the case.

It appears that we are no longer permitted to
use the old adage, that " exceptions prove the
rule "; nevertheless, when these solitary instances
are strongly insisted upon, we can but feel that it
would not be so much a matter of comment for
a few actors to be well received, if it were not
altogether customary to taboo the majority.

I am making myself now the mouthpiece of a
class of people ; its " shining lights," like the shining lights of other classes, require no champion.

But the point is here : it is not *the good* in
whose favor distinctions are made in America,
but *the great.*

Players like those alluded to are quietly segre-
gated from the ranks in which they belong, and
the bulk of the profession remains under the social ban.

I hope yet to see the day when actors and actresses shall be judged by their deserts, and when

it shall be no longer customary to make decent and worthy men and women share the odium which is cast upon the stage by the representatives of the naked, the indecent, or the Drunken Drama.

VII.

HE Drunken Drama has two branches. One branch is illustrated by the actor who represents drunkenness on the stage, as he might represent thievery, murder, or any other wickedness. The other branch is illustrated by the actor who gets drunk.

Not infrequently the two are combined, and Toodles on the stage is also Toodles in private. He may move us to laughter in the theatre, but we may be assured there will be others whom he will move to tears out of it.

It was formerly more common than it is now to endeavor to make the drama subservient to the cause of temperance: such plays as *The Drunkard* and *Ten Nights in a Bar-Room* were used as a means of warning to young men. Now, the

8 *

serious drunkard has gone out of fashion, and his place in the drama is occupied by such amusing sots as Toodles and Eccles. When the play of *The Drunkard* was first produced, it created a marked sensation. Its chief impersonator, a delicate young man of twenty-five, named Goodall, died of excessive drinking, and the piece expired with its great representative.

Goodall was an extraordinary example of the preacher who fails to practise his own precepts. There may have been those who profited by his "fearful example," as nightly rendered to crowded houses. I have heard some very impressive stories to that effect, but never gave them much credit; but the actor himself was not warned.

The personation was no mere mimicry with Goodall. He himself had felt the anguish he so powerfully portrayed.

But the bitterest comment on the influence of such representations remains in the fact, that although this unhappy young man reformed on the stage every night during a period of three years, he never extended his reformation into private life.

They call this sort of play "the moral drama." The term is a ridiculous one, and one born of cant.

Aside from its absurdity, it is an insult to every other class of dramatic production, and I can only wonder that any self-respecting manager should ever have adopted it.

It implies that the drama proper is immoral. That position is one which should be left for the enemies of the theatre to assume.

I have a sincere respect for genuine convictions, and a sincere contempt for narrow prejudice. It is to mere prejudice that the original inventor of the "moral drama" pandered; and, by doing so, tacitly admitted that such prejudices were well founded.

It is rather extraordinary, to one who looks for candor in opponents of the stage, that they should take its abuses as a basis on which to form a judgment of the stage itself. I do not now recall any other branch of art that is thus ill-treated.

Not long ago, the novel was the sharer of the stage in this sort of denunciation, but it is so no longer. A distinction is made between the good and the bad, not alone among novels, but *in* novels; and works which twenty years ago would have been eyed askance by many good people are now permitted to lie upon their family tables, and are read around the evening lamp.

This is not because the novels have changed, but because the sentiment of the religious world has changed.

Our mothers can remember when "Oliver Twist" and the "Pickwick Papers" were not deemed fit to be read in strictly guarded circles. To-day, the same circles — that is, the same style of people, with the same habits of morality and the same religious convictions — do not taboo even the works of that dreadful Mr. Thackeray, who has done for morality and honor so splendid a work.

There are abuses, vices, wickednesses connected with the stage; but the stage is not an abuse, a vice, nor a wickedness. Its evils I am going to labor all my life, in my humble way, to try and right. But I am at the same time going to continue a defender of THE DRAMA, with voice and pen, always and everywhere.

There- has been a deal of stupid talk in this world about the "warning influence" of plays which hold the mirror up to vice. This also is born of cant.

We have heard of thievishly-inclined apprentices being "warned" from putting their fingers into their employer's cash-box by witnessing the career of George Barnwell. We have been told of terrible creatures, who were ripe for murder, being so horror-stricken over the woes of Macbeth that they immediately put on a clean shirt and joined the church.

All stuff!

I contend that it is just here we may all look for the worst influence of the play-house. The "leg-business" is trivial in comparison with the "moral drama," so far as its bad influence upon auditors is concerned.

These horrible representations of vice ought to be banished the stage. Those people are wholly in error who believe their influence to be beneficial. The same people believe that the spectacle of a murderer murdered by the law's hand, dangling hideously between earth and sky at a

rope's end, is a useful one to the spectators; and
that the column-length printing of the records
of crime in the newspapers, in prurient detail,
exerts a moral influence.

These things are horrible and pernicious in
their influence. The stage should be swept of
them.

The influence of the stage on morality is a
clear one, but the censors do not seem to know
wherein it lies. Nobody goes to the theatre to
be preached to. The prime object of the theatre
is to entertain, and it is for the purpose of being
entertained that people go there.

The first aim of even the "moral drama" is to
entertain; and, if it fail in that, nobody will go
to see it.

But by making the amusement pure and beautiful in itself, the theatre insensibly exerts a good
influence.

It is not necessary to preach morality, but to
exhibit amusing, refining, and agreeable phases of
life — real life — that we may not be disgusted
with human nature.

The dramatist who goes out of his way to

inculcate a moral does an unprofitable thing.
It is the *tone* that runs through a play which
renders it beneficial.

It stirs to laughter, or sympathetic tears. It
touches the chords of sweet emotions in the spectators. When it curdles their blood with horror,
makes them shiver, it is as pernicious and hateful
as when it directly panders to vice.

These opinions are only the result of careful
and thoughtful observation, not of any philo-
sophic theory. I am neither philosopher nor
moralist; but, like Mr. Emerson, I can "say
what I see." I can not prove myself right, in
any logical and altogether crushing way. But,
womanlike, I can ask a question, and I will:—

Who most love the so-called "moral drama"?'
The Bowery boys.

Who cheer the loudest at a melodramatic and
high-sounding moral "gag" from an actor's
tongue? The little rascals of the Old Bowery
pit, who would pick your pocket without a
scruple.

"Ha-a-a, villun!" roars the gallant young sailor
in immaculate white trowsers and kid slippers,

"I have unmasked ye! Begone, villun! and know — aha! — that he who would lie to his wife would not hesuttate to rob a bank of millions!"

And "hi! hi!" shout the dirty little gallery gods. They like it; it suits their ideas exactly; but be careful they do not get too near you when you are leaving the theatre, or your pocketbook may change owners.

Go to some profounder metaphysician than I am for an explanation of why this is so. But rest assured that it *is* so. If there be any exceptions to prove the rule, I hope you know of them. I do not.

But while the "moral" drunken drama is hurtful in an indirect and not easily explainable way, the representation of drunkenness in its comic aspect is hurtful in an equal, perhaps a greater degree, and in a way that is quite comprehensible.

Man is a monkey in his penchant for imitation, and he especially loves to imitate that which is funny. The boys at the circus go home and imitate the clown, mimic his antics, retail his jokes; and, if they arouse a laugh thereby, are elated with their success. They mimic Toodles and Eccles in the same way.

Men — who are but grown-up boys — are inspired by the same spirit. They get a great idea of the humorous aspect of drunkenness, and they do not shrink from exhibiting it in their own persons to a choice circle of their fellows. They get drunk over dinners at Delmonico's, and mock Toodles in a way that makes their companions, themselves a little drunk also, laugh uproariously.

They go into bar-rooms, slap each other hilariously on the back, jam their hats on the backs of their heads, and mock old Eccles.

Spectators and amateur performers are here under the influence of the same baneful thing — the idea that Eccles and Toodles are funny off the stage as well as on.

And so they are; and the drunkard off the stage sometimes provokes the spirit of imitation too, no doubt. There are all sorts of pernicious influences at work in the world. I would keep them out of all literature, whether in novels or in plays.

9

Of course the most deplorable branch of the drunken drama is that which is illustrated by the actor who gets drunk.

The most vicious feature of this branch, strangely enough, is often presented by the audience.

No theatre-goer can have failed to note the bad influence the audience sometimes exerts in its manner of treating the actor who is addicted to liquor in private life. His vice really seems in some mysterious way to make him a favorite. Instances of this are painfully abundant.

An actor, now in the height of his popularity, who is known to be sadly intemperate, finds himself greeted by enthusiastic applause whenever he has occasion, in his assumed character, to allude to drinking in a humorous way.

Eight or ten years ago, in a Western town, my sister was one night summoned to play in the *Lady of Lyons.* The house was all sold, a large and fashionable audience was gathered, and expectation was on tiptoe.

Eight o'clock arrived; the curtain remained down; the audience became impatient. There was trouble behind the scenes. No Claude Melnotte was to be found. The actor above alluded to was cast for the part, but he had not come.

"Where can he be?" was anxiously asked by Pauline. "Oh, I know where to find him," replied the manager. "Johnny will be sure to be . at the faro-table, and drunk."

His words were verified. "Johnny" *was* at the faro-table, — and drunk. By some subtle system of telegraphy, the audience became aware of this fact; but, so far from being indignant at it, when the greatly-belated Johnny at length stepped on the stage, his appearance was the signal for a burst of enthusiastic approbatory yells, which changed into decided applause when Johnny thickly stumbled over the first speech of Bulwer's hero.

Johnny has manfully sustained his reputation for faro-playing and drunkenness during the past ten years, and it was only the other night that I heard him enthusiastically sustained by applause when he announced that the wine-cup was a trinket with which he was quite at home — or words to that effect.

Johnny is still young, handsome, graceful, and of such decided talent for dramatic art that he occasionally trenches on actual genius. It is very sad to see his leaning to drink, but it is even sadder to see how his audiences encourage him in it.

Another example of this kind was furnished by a well-known actor who died recently in a distant State. He was the most charming Romeo I ever saw; and, when he chose to vary, where so delightful a Mercutio as he? Frequently he addressed the audience when very drunk.

I remember on one occasion, in Philadelphia, his coming down to the footlights and saying, — " Ladies and gentlemen, d'ye see that man? He ought t' be pardoned. I, being the Duke, ought t' pardon him, but our property-man is *such a drunkard* that he hasn't put one speck of pardon on the table."

If this speech had been hissed, it might have been a rebuke strong enough to bring about the reformation of the unfortunate actor (for there was never a man so apprehensive of the displeasure of an audience); but, on the contrary, it

seemed to afford universal amusement and grati-
-fication.

Few of my readers are ignorant of the fact
that the elder Booth, whose like we shall not see
again, was often intoxicated while playing.
Strangely enough, *his* artistic powers were as
strong when he was in that state as when he was
quite sober. Many aver that his sober Richard
was a tame and puerile thing compared to the
noisy Gloster of perhaps a hundred cups.

It seems, however, scarcely necessary to add
that when in this state Booth's brain was no
clearer than that of another man who is intoxicated; and, though he managed to give his grand
"points" with perhaps even greater force than
when he was sober, he effectually ruined the play
for all the other performers, and in the main,
for the audience.

When I was a little girl, Booth was once playing, in conjunction with my sister, in Memphis,
and she sent me one night to deliver some
message to him on the stage.

The curtain had not yet risen, but I found Mr.
Booth standing at the back of the stage, inside

9 *

the tomb of the Capulets, for the nonce unoccupied by any defunct member of that illustrious house.

I approached timidly, and delivered my message; whereupon, starting up with the graceful spring of a tiger disturbed, he hissed out, —

"Avaunt, and quit my sight! Let the earth hide thee!
Thy bones are marrowless, thy blood is cold;
Thou hast no speculation in those eyes
Which thou dost glare with!"

Any one who has seen Booth, and remembers the terrible intensity of his voice, the wonderful *crescendo* which he placed on the word *gla-a-are!* in this sentence, will not be surprised to learn that a weak, sickly little girl, as I was, should have toppled straight over in a dead swoon at hearing it so unexpectedly and unjustly addressed to herself, in the semi-darkness of the Capulet tomb.

It is needless to say that the great tragedian was intoxicated.

On this occasion, after I had been discovered, and a couch had been extemporized for me in my sister's dressing-room, I remember hearing such peals on peals of applause for his acting that I lay there in an agonized fear that he would add further to my distresses by playing so well that the audience would tear the house down in their enthusiasm.

The next time I saw Booth he was playing with Miss Davenport (Mrs. Lander). The piece was *The Apostate*, and on this occasion I formed one of the audience.

The reader who is familiar with this play will remember where Alvarez gives Florinda to Hemeya, who, receiving her with applause, exclaims, "Who now shall part us?"

At this moment on strode the terrible Pescara, and roared the one word, "I!"

Booth was intoxicated again! And his whole bearing so reminded me of the previous occasion when he had given me a fright from which I had not yet fully recovered, that, forgetting decorum and everything else, I started up from my seat and rushed pell-mell out of the theatre.

On several occasions I saw Edwin Booth, a tall, slender boy, who seemed all eyes, standing behind

the scenes intently watching his father's performances, and I remember wondering if the little
boy's father ever frightened him as he had
frightened me.

Hissing in theatres is no longer practised in
this country, save in the rarest instances.   There
are other modes of expressing disapproval which
are quite as effectual, perhaps, and it is not
desirable that hissing should be resorted to,
except in case of the gravest offence.

Such offence, I think, is afforded by the actor
who appears drunk on the stage.   It is an insult
to his audience, and the audience has a right to
resent it as such.

I doubt if there be an actor living who would
not become speedily cured of this vice if the
audience took that course with him.   The cure
might not extend to private life, it is true; but
that, so far as the interests of art are concerned,
is a secondary consideration.

I know no reason why an actor's *private* vices
should be taken in hand by the public in any
way that they would not be if he were not an
actor.   It is solely in the interests of art that

I am writing now; and art requires that its
devotees should not put an enemy in their
mouths to steal away their brains.

I wonder if there be any one among the cen-
surers of the stage who will find in the drunkenness of occasional actors another proof of the
wickedness of the whole profession?

I wonder if it will be argued that this article is
a concession to the prejudices of these worthy
people, and an argument ready-made for their
use?

Perhaps I ought not to wonder, but to take it
for granted that such a course of reasoning will
be adopted. Even more untenable positions than
this are continually taken. In fact, the only
ground the opponent of the theatre can walk on ·
is found in the faults that are connected with it
— faults which no one deplores more heartily
than I do. I admit that some actors drink —
ergo, " actors are a dreadful set of people."

But do not some orators drink? I once saw
a Fourth of July orator so tipsy that he could

hardly stand straight while he mumbled his oration.

I know of a celebrated lecturer and college professor who has a glass of liquor on the desk before him, and never lectures except in a condition of mild intoxication.

Do you therefore pronounce oratory a wickedness, and orators a "dreadful set"?

Do not literary men drink? I have heard, it seems to me, of Bohemians who were in that habit, who yet did not succeed in casting a stigma on all literature by their vice,—whose books are read in the purest circles, and noticed favorably in the most rigid journals.

Do not statesmen drink? The annals of statesmanship present many dreadful examples of brilliant intellects besotted by liquor, and of mediocre men tipsy in high office. Do you condemn statesmanship therefore?

Do not hod-carriers drink? Do you condemn hod-carrying therefore?

If I could always as easily foresee the position the learned gentleman on the other side would take, I should be glad; but his positions are often so much more untenable than this that it seems a waste of energy to answer them at all.

I claim for actors and actresses in private life precisely what is claimed for men and women in every other calling, — that they shall be esteemed according to their merits as men and women. If they are virtuous and honorable, their virtue and honor should be recognized, approved, and encouraged, even by those who disapprove of their calling.

The concert-singer, the professional pianist — all, in fact, who live by music, exist in an atmosphere precisely like that of the actor, but they do not share his odium in the eyes of Mrs. Grundy.

I repeat that the claim is for consideration of private merit or demerit, without regard to occupation.

An actor who leads a correct life is deserving of the same good name, and the same social recognition, as the painter who does the same.

An actress who leads an immoral life is by no just man to be held up as a proof that the drama is immoral, any more than a poetess who does the same is to cast a stigma upon all poesy.

" Of all classes," says the *American Cyclopæ-dia*, " they (actors and actresses) are the freest from crime." For an actor to figure in a criminal trial, or to inhabit a prison, always has been a thing so rare that it is observed and commented on in the same marked manner as crimes among clergymen are.

Where crime is rare, it is a sign of the excellence of the class.

Intemperance is generally the worst vice these people have; and all the other features of vice are so little known among them that this one stands out with undue prominence, and is universally exaggerated and overdrawn.

While I deplore its existence, too, I deny that it prevails to the extent commonly claimed, and I assert that it prevails to a *greater* extent among the people who arrogate to themselves the title of " our best society."

I speak of what I know, and not as one who has simply heard from an outside place. I have moved in the " highest circles," and I have moved in theatrical circles, and *I know*.

If it were not a course altogether too contemptible for my self-respect to approve of, I could unmask the private lives of many who are received freely in the "highest circles," and show that they furnish a parallel to the very worst lives of players, — even extending the sphere of the player, for the nonce, so that it shall include those indecent women who disgrace our dramatic temples with the orgies of the Leg Business.

IX.

ABOUT THE LEG BUSINESS.

WO classes of "female" performers are associated with the " naked drama," as it has been called. The first are a legitimate branch of the theatrical profession, and in their way may be, and often are, artists. They are the ballet-dancers.

The theatre as legitimately deals in music and dancing as it does in tragedy or comedy. Hence, the ballet is, and always has been, as freely recognized by the most cultured people (when they approve of the theatre at all) as any other feature of the mimic world.

For the dancers of the legitimate ballet, I — who know them as a class well — have some respect. They are for the most part a hard-working, ill-paid body of women, not infrequently the sole support of entire families, and their moral characters are not one whit affected by their line of business.

The admiring public which sees the pretty picture they make on the stage little knows the physical fatigue which these poor girls encounter in return for a few dollars a week salary from the manager, and an illiberal judgment at the hands of the audience.

Few men work so hard as the ballet-girl — the coryphée, who, by half-past eight in the morning, is at the theatre, clad in gauze and silk webbing, practising pirouettes, entrechats, the toe-torture, and other inquisitorial exercises.

I have seen these girls practise from nine o'clock in the morning until half-past twelve, almost without cessation; then take a hurried lunch, sometimes eating it while standing shivering in their thin clothing in a draughty space behind the "flats," only to begin their labor again at half-past one, and so continue till five.

This is for the matinee performance; at half-past seven that of the night commences, finishing perhaps at eleven.

Then comes undressing, re-dressing, folding and laying away their stage paraphernalia; for, even if not naturally tidy (and tidiness is the rule with them, the exceptions rare) these girls must, for economy's sake, be careful of their clothing.

And so, long after midnight, the tired creatures, often laden with heavy bundles, creep listlessly into street cars, to be stared at by rude men, or, still worse, drag home through the deserted streets, alone and unprotected, at risk of being mistaken for *traviatas* of the lowest grade.

With the dancer who has passed the chrysalis ballet-girl stage, and is now a full fledged butterfly *première*, with her name large-lettered in the bills, and her engagement-papers stamped and signed at the lawyer's, the road is not so stony.

I am far from placing the ballet-girl in the same rank with an intellectual player; but there are grades of quality in all fields. She is a dancer, and loves dancing as an art. That pose into which she now throws herself with such abandon is not a vile pandering to the taste of those giggling men in the orchestra-stalls, but is an effort which, to her idea, is as loving a tribute to a beloved art as a painter's dearest pencil-touch is to him.

I have seen these women burst into tears on leaving the stage because they had observed men laughing among themselves, rolling their eyes about, and evidently making unworthy comments on the pretty creature before them, whose whole heart was for the hour lovingly given over to Terpsichore.

" It is *they* who are bad," said Mademoiselle B. to me the other night; " it is not we."

Those men who have impure thoughts are the persons on whom censure should fall, not upon the devotees of an art which the dancers love, and embody to the best of their ability, and without any more idea of impurity because of the dress, which is both the conventional and the only practicable one, than sculptors or painters have when they use the female figure as a medium to convey their ideas of poetry to the outside world.

But there is one set of exponents of the

10 *

"naked drama" on whom I am for launching every possible invective of censure and reproach.

I mean those women who are "neither fish, flesh, nor fowl" of the theatrical creation,—who are neither actresses, pantomimists, nor ballet-girls, but who enjoy a celebrity more widely spread than many legitimate artists could hope to attain.

It is unpleasant to mention names; it is disagreeable and even dangerous to do so; but when such women as Cora Pearl, Vestvali, Menken, and their like were insolent enough to invade the stage, and involve in the obloquy which falls on them hundreds of good and pure women, it was time for even the most tolerant critic to express disapprobation.

Whatever the private character of these women might be,—however good, however bad,—we were justified, from their public exhibitions, in denouncing them as shameless and unworthy.

It is true, they made more money than any other class of "performers;" more money than the poetic Edwin Booth; infinitely more than the intellectual E. L. Davenport.

Stifle conscience, honor, and decency, and mere money-making is easy work, as these women and others who have come later fully illustrate.

In this chapter, whose main facts were set down before the fever for "blonde burlesque" raged in our theatres, I treat principally of a style of performance which the above-named women illustrate, and which is already fluttering in the last agonies of death. But so long as it lives, however sickly, my denunciation of the women who illustrate it has "excuse for being." These women are not devotees of any art. With the exception of Vestvali — a failure on every lyric stage, both in Europe and America, — they do not either act, dance, sing, or mime ; but they habit themselves in a way which is attractive to an indelicate taste, and their inefficiency in other regards is overlooked.

Some of these women, strange as it may seem, have occasional aspirations for higher things.

A play which I prepared for the stage in the year 186– had for its heroine a woman of tender feelings, holy passions, such as every author loves to paint.

After its production at one of the theatres in Broadway, I had many applicants for the purchase of copies. Among these applicants was a person whose name is thoroughly associated with the Mazeppa, Dick Turpin, Jack Sheppard school, and none other.

I was astonished that such a woman could covet such a part. What sympathy had the "French spy" with a heroine, tearful, suffering, and self-denying? What was the chastening influence of anguish and repentance to Jack Sheppard and his jolly pals who "fake away" so obstreperously in the burden of the chorus, and the pockets of the unwary?

I could not help expressing my astonishment at this seeming inconsistency to a person who was acquainted with my applicant, for I was not.

"Well, you see," he replied, referring to her familiarly, by her *petit nom*, "Leo hates the leg business as much as anybody; but, bless you, nothing else pays nowadays, — so what can she do?"

The leg business is a business which requires legs.

That these should be naturally symmetrical is desirable, but not indispensable; for the art of padding has reached such perfection, that nature has been almost distanced, and stands, blushing at her own incompetency, in the background.

New York can boast some artistic "padders;" and, if you are curious to know where they dwell, what their prices are, etc., you can go to almost any green-room of this period, and find their business cards stuck about in the frames of the looking-glasses, in the joints of the gas-burners, and sometimes lying on the top of the sacred cast-case itself.

Strange to say, however, that Holy of Holies, the city of Philadelphia, bears off the palm in the pad-making art. Thus the New Jersey railroads are frequently enriched by the precious freight of penitential Mazeppas, going on pilgrimages to the padding Mecca.

It is generally supposed — by those who suppose anything at all on the subject — that padding is employed only in the enlarging and beautifying of the calf of the leg, but this is a mistake.

Such little inaccuracies as knock-knees, and bow-legs — trifling errata in Nature's original edition, remarkable for their frequency in the human family, and especially in those misguided members of it who have rashly chosen the stage as a profession — are nimbly rectified by the pad-professor.

I saw a letter from one of these the other day, which may be worth producing here for the sake of its ludicrousness. That it is a genuine document, I pledge my word. It ran thus, —

"PHILADELFIA.

"MAM: — Them tites is finished your nees will be all O K when you get them on. Bad figgers is all plaid out now they will caust 9 dollers."

It would seem that the nine dollars capital, a couple of yards of white muslin, and the outer "tites," are all that is required of the followers of the Mazeppa school.

Of personal beauty, they have often little;

of intellectuality, of comprehension, of grace, genius, poetry, less; and of talent, none.

When the part they portray calls for the speaking of words, we lift our hands in blank astonishment that any creature with audacity enough to assume such a position can have so little ability to fill it.

The money the Mazeppas make is something quite astonishing. Ten thousand dollars "share" for a month's engagement was paid but a short time ago to one of the most attractive of the "French spies." In less than two months after, she was obliged to borrow money to pay her hotel bill.

"Easy come, easy go," is a proverb which must have been made for these women.

It is not strange, perhaps, that they should have implicit faith in the potency of King Greenback, and offer him with little delicacy, to gain that always-desired end,— flattering comments in the newspapers.

I have an editorial friend, of an extremely conscientious turn of mind, who was coolly asked by a Mazeppa if he would not take up the cudgels of criticism for her, as against another local paper, at the same time drawing from her pocket an immense roll of bills, and asking him to "take what he wanted." He complied with her request; for he wanted *nothing* that savored of bribery, and he took "what he wanted."

There are those who understand rather better the delicate art of administering the critic-douceur.

One such, on coming to New York for the first time, hearing that to mollify Muggins was indispensable to her success, sat down, after much deliberation, and mailed him a black letter, or blackmailed him a white letter, inclosing a fifty-dollar bill, and a transparent cloak for bribery in the shape of a request that he would send her one stanza of a song of his own brilliant composition (he having never written a line of verse in his life), leaving the subject, air, metre and sentiment open to his discriminating judgment.

The fifty-dollar bill was never heard of more; but the four lines of tender thought which follow were sent to her address,—

Air. — "*I know a bank*" (*note.*)
Come, love, come, where the roses blow,
And the angels tune their radiant hair,
Where the zephyrs sigh to the far-off zones,
And the sleeping seas swell on the air.

How's that?

If the stage could but be rid of the "leg business" scourge, there is no reason why it should
not form a worthy channel for gifted, intelligent,
and virtuous young women to gain a livelihood
through. But in its present condition — overrun
as it is by troops of immodest women — there is,
alas! but little encouragement to any woman
who respects herself to turn to the stage for
support.

Openings for women are few enough, as gov-
ernesses, and schoolmistresses, and shirtmakers,
and hoopskirt drudges, generally, will testify.

But worse slavery than any or all of these is
the thraldom of waiting to be married to have
one's board and lodging paid.

, A woman should have her destiny in her own
hands as completely as a man has his, and the
first boon that should be vouchsafed her is the

11

happy knowledge that, before she lies down at night, she may really thank her Maker, and not her husband, for having given her this day her daily bread.

X.

ABOUT NUDITY IN THEATRES.

"NUDE. Bare." — *Webster.*
"BARE. Wanting clothes, or ill-supplied with garments."— *Johnson.*

THERE were always great evils attaching to the theatrical profession. I have always deplored them deeply. Some of them I have touched upon in the preceding chapters. No one who has read my articles, or listened to my lectures, will say that I have not earnestly defended the theatrical profession, — as such. I have also said, honestly, how I loathe the evils which attach to it. In this feeling of loathing, I have expressed the sentiments of a large class of people who were, like myself, bred to the stage, but who could not shut their eyes to the evils referred to.

Within a few years, these evils had grown to appalling dimensions. Decency and virtue had been crowded from the ranks by indecency and licentiousness. A coarse rage for nudity had spread in our theatres, until it had come to be the ruling force in them.

Seeing this truth, I shuddered at it. Seeing its effects, I mourned over them. In every place where I spoke of the stage, I denounced this encroaching shame; but I always coupled with denunciation of it defence of THE DRAMA.

At the Woman's Suffrage Convention in New York, in May, 1869, I denounced this thing again; but, as I was not speaking at length upon this subject, but only touched upon it in passing, and by way of illustration, I did not, as usual, defend THE DRAMA.

At once, there rose so wild a yell, as all the fiends from heaven that fell were furious at my course.

Certain portions of the press attacked me, and accused me of slandering the profession to which I once belonged. Anonymous letters poured in upon me at the office of the Authors' Union in a sort of flood, villifying me, upbraiding me, covering me with coarse and gross revilings.

I was asked to explain such base conduct. It was demanded that I should take back my rash and reckless statements. I was requested to remember that I had once been very glad to think well of the theatrical profession. How *dared* I say I could advise no honorable woman to turn to the stage for support?

In a word, I was put upon my defence.

Turning the matter over in my mind carefully, I came to the conclusion that I had in my hands an opportunity for doing a great deal of good by the simple course of making my defence.

And I concluded, also, that my testimony in this matter had peculiar weight, as coming from one who is of a dramatic family, and may be presumed to speak from close and immediate observation, if not from experience.

I, therefore, wrote the words which follow; and, in reproducing them here, I shall only express the sincere hope that when this book is read, the evil here treated of will be so much a

11 *

thing of the past, that this chapter shall possess no other value than as a record of a dark page in the history of the theatre.

Though for some years I have not played a part in a theatre, I have 'not been altogether separated from association with its people. The ties which bind me to these people are strong and close. I never expect to sever them wholly; but they shall never prevent me from giving my allegiance to the cause of morality, virtue, honor, and integrity, though, as a consequence of this, the theatrical heavens fall.

That curse of the dramatic profession, for which editors, critics, authors, and managers struggle to find a fitting name, is my general theme in this article; which is, at the same time, my defence against the charge of slandering the dramatic profession.

What the *Tribune* calls the Dirty Drama, the *World* the Nude Drama, the *Times* the Leg Drama, and other journals various other expressive adjective styles of *drama*, I call the Leg *Business*, simply.

Does any one call the caperings of a tight-rope performer the Ærial Drama? — the tricks of an educated hog the Porcine Drama?

There is a term in use among "professionals" which embraces all sorts of performances in its comprehensiveness, to wit: The Show Business.

In this term is included every possible thing which is of the nature of an entertainment, with these three requirements: 1. A place of gathering. 2. An admission fee. 3. An audience.

This remarkably comprehensive term covers with the same mantle the tragic Forrest, when he plays; the comic Jefferson, when *he* plays; the eloquent Beecher, when he lectures; and the sweet-voiced Parepa, when she sings. It also covers with the same mantle the wandering juggler, who balances feathers on his nose; the gymnast, who whirls on a trapeze; the danseuse, who interprets the poetry of motion; the clown, who cracks stale jokes in the ring; the performer on the tight-rope, the negro minstrel, the giant and the dwarf, the learned pig, and the educated monkey. Therefore, it includes the clog-dancing creature, with yellow hair and indecent costume.

All these things being included in the show business, you see it is almost as wide a world as the outer world. It must be a very wide world which should include Mr. Beecher with the learned pig.

It must be a very wide world which should include Rachel, Ristori, Janauschek, and Lander with the clog-dancing creature of indecent action and attire.

But, by as good a right as you would call Mr. Beecher and the learned pig performers in the intellectual sphere, you would call Janauschek and the clog-dancing creature interpreters of THE DRAMA.

How, then, does it happen that in attacking these yellow-haired nudities, I am compelled to · say that they disgrace the dramatic profession?

In this wise: These creatures occupy the temples of the drama; they perform in conjunction with actors and actresses, on the same stage, before the same audience, in the same hour. They are made legitimate members of our theatrical companies, and take part in those nondescript performances which are called burlesques, spectacles, what you will. They carry off the chief honors of the hour; their names occupy the chief places on the bills; and, as I said in my speech at the Equal Rights Meeting at Steinway Hall, they win the chief prizes in the theatrical world.

A woman, who has not ability enough to rank as a passable "walking lady" in a good theatre, on a salary of twenty-five dollars a week, can strip herself almost naked, and be thus qualified to go upon the stage of two-thirds of our theatres at a salary of one hundred dollars and upwards.

Clothed in the dress of an honest woman, she is worth nothing to a manager. Stripped as naked as she dare — and it seems there is little left when so much is done — she becomes a prize to her manager, who knows that crowds will rush to see her, and who pays her a salary accordingly.

These are simple facts, which permit of no denial. I doubt if there is a manager in the land who would dream of denying them.

There are certain accomplishments which render the Nude Woman "more valuable to managers in the degree that she possesses them." I will tell you what these accomplishments are, and you shall judge how far they go toward making her, in any true sense, an actress.

They are: 1. The ability to sing. 2. The ability to jig. 3. The ability to play on certain musical instruments.

Now that I have put them down, I perceive that they need explanation, after all; so complete is the perversion of everything pertaining to this theme, that the very language is beggared of its power of succinct expression.

To sing. Yes, but not to sing as Parepa sings; nor such songs as she sings. The songs in demand in this sphere are vulgar, senseless — and, to be most triumphantly successful, should be capable of indecent constructions, and accompanied by the wink, the wriggle, the grimace, which are not peculiar to virtuous women, whatever else they are. The more senseless the song, the more utterly it is idiotic drivel, the better it will answer in the absence of the baser requisites. Here is a specimen:

> "Little Bo-peep, she lost her sheep,
> And don't know where to fi-*ind* her;
> Leave her alone and she'll come home,
> And fetch her tail behi-*ind* her."

A simple nursery song; and, if men were babies, innocent and harmless in itself; but men are not babies, and the song is not sung in a simple or harmless manner, but with the wink or the idiotic stare that means a world, and sets the audience into an extatic roaring.

To jig. Let no one confound jig-dancing with the poetry of motion which is illustrated by a thoroughly organized and thorough-bred body of ballet-dancers.

Ballet-dancing is a profession by itself, just as distinctly as is singing in opera. A danseuse, like Fanny Ellsler or Taglioni, or, to come to the present moment, like Morlacchi, is no more to be ranked with these nude jiggers than an actress like Mrs. Lander is.

The ability to jig is an accomplishment which

any of these nude creatures can pick up in a few weeks. A danseuse, who has any claim whatever to the title of *artiste,* must be bred to her profession through years of toil and study.

In this country, the ballet proper has had little illustration. Yet it is a branch of art, — not the noblest art, it is true; but, by the side of the jigging woman, almost rising to dignity.

To play on certain musical instruments. These instruments should be such as to look queer in a woman's hands, — such instruments as the banjo and the bugle.

Now, I am not saying that the ability to sing silly songs, to jig, or to play the banjo, in itself disgraces a woman, however little it may entitle her to my esteem. I am only calling attention to them as valuable aids to the nude woman in her business, and letting you judge whether they give her any right to the name of *actress.*

You, no doubt, will at once remark that these accomplishments have hitherto been peculiar to that branch of the show business occupied by the negro minstrel. But in the hands of the negro minstrel, these accomplishments amuse us without disgusting us. They are not wedded to bare legs, indecent wriggles, nor suggestive feminine leers and winks; nor is there a respectable minstrel band in the United States to-day which would tolerate in its members the *double entendres* which fly about the stages of some of the largest temples of the drama in this city. The minstrels would not dare utter them. Their halls would be vacated, and their business ruined. It requires that a half-naked woman should utter these ribaldrous inuendoes, before our fastidious public will receive them unrebukingly.

To what branch of the show business, then, do these creatures belong? .

I answer, to that branch which is known by the names of variety-show, concert-saloon, music-hall, and various other titles, which mean nothing unless you already know what they mean.

No one in the show business needs to be told what a variety-show is. It certainly is not a theatre.

Until the reign of the nude woman set in, variety-halls were the resort of only the lowest

12

and vilest, and women were not seen in the audience.

The nude woman was sometimes seen upon the stage, but she was only one of a large variety of attractions, — she was a tid-bit, hugely relished by the low and vile who went to see her; but only permitted to exhibit herself economically, for fear of cloying the public appetite.

Delicate caution! but how useless, her later career in our theatres has shown.

There, she is exhibited ceaselessly for three hours, in every variety which an indecent imagination can devise.

When the *Black Crook* first presented its nude woman to the gaze of a crowded auditory, she was met with a gasp of astonishment at the effrontery which dared so much. Men actually grew pale at the boldness of the thing; a death-like silence fell over the house, broken only by the clapping of a band of *claqueurs* around the outer aisles; but it passed; and, in view of the fact that these women were French ballet-dancers after all, they were tolerated.

By slow and almost imperceptible degrees, this

shame has grown, until to-day the indecency of that exhibition is far surpassed. Those women were ballet-dancers from France and Italy, and they represented in their nudity imps and demons. In silence they whirled about the stage; in silence trooped off. Some faint odor of ideality and poetry rested over them.

The nude woman of to-day represents nothing but herself. She runs upon the stage giggling; trots down to the foot-lights, winks at the audience, rattles off from her tongue some stupid attempts at wit, some twaddling allusions to Sorosis, or General Grant, or other subject prominent in the public eye, and is always peculiarly and emphatically herself, — the woman, that is, whose name is on the bills in large letters, and who considers herself an object of admiration to the spectators.

The sort of ballet-dancer who figured in the *Black Crook* is paralleled on the stage of every theatre in this city, except one, at this time.

She no longer excites attention.

To create a proper and profitable sensation in the breast of man, she no longer suffices. Something bolder must be devised, — something that shall utterly eclipse and outstrip her.

Hence, the nude woman of to-day, — who outstrips her in the broadest sense. And, as if it were not enough that she should be allowed to go unhissed and unrotten-egged, she must be baptized with the honors of a profession for which Shakespeare wrote!

Managers recognize her as an actress, and pay her sums ranging from fifty to a thousand dollars a week, according to her value in their eyes. Actresses, who love virtue better than money, are driven into the streets by her; and it becomes a grave and solemn question with hundreds of honorable women what they shall do to earn a livelihood.

I say it is nothing less than an insult to the members of the dramatic profession, that these nude women should be classed among actresses and hold possession of the majority of our theatres. Their place is in the concert-saloons or the circus tents. Theatres are for artists.

A friend said to me the other day that it was inconsistent in me to find indecency in women exposing their persons, when men constantly do the same; that, as an honest exponent of Woman's Rights, I ought to see no more immodesty in a woman dancing a jig in flesh-colored ¬ leggings than in a man performing a circus feat in the same costume.

I reply, that I think such shows are indecent in both sexes. Yet, nevertheless, in woman a thousand times more indecent than in man; for the simple reason, that the costume of the sexes in every-day life is different.

To ignore this fact is to just wilfully shut one's eyes to a reasonable argument.

Women in society conceal all the lower part of their bodies with drapery, — and for good and sufficient reasons, which no man, who has a wife or mother, should stop to question.

But set this aside. Circus men, who strip to the waist in this fashion, don't claim to be actors.

Now, I come back to the words I said at the Woman Suffrage Convention. They have been variously reported by the newspapers. They were exactly as follows, —

12 *

"I can advise no honorable, self-respecting woman to turn to the stage for support, with its demoralizing influences, which seem to be growing stronger and stronger day by day; where the greatest rewards are won by a set of brazen-faced, clog-dancing creatures, with dyed yellow hair and padded limbs, who have come here in droves from across the ocean."

I have been astonished and pained at the extent to which the meaning of these words has been distorted. The press and my anonymous letter critics seem to be agreed in taking the view, that I attack, in these words, the profession in which I was reared, and all my family.

Some of the letters sent me are from religious people, encouraging me to go on; others are from actors and actresses, seeking to dissuade me, — not always in gentle language.

The first letter on which I lay my hands, so gross in its language that I suspect it to be from one of the nude women themselves, says, —

"You were, no doubt, satisfied with the stage so long as it paid. Now, don't swear at the bridge that carried you over."

Perhaps this person, being new to the country, thinks it is true, as a newspaper once said, that I was formerly a ballet-girl.

Hitherto, I have only laughed at this story, as on a par with that of the person who thought me a daughter of the negro preacher, Loguen; or that of the " dress reform " scarecrow, who believed me " formerly a ballad songstress."

I laugh at it no longer. I answer, in all gravity, that I never was a ballet-girl, nor even a jig-dancer.

It is true that I was once a member of the theatrical profession; so were my father and my mother; so were my five sisters; but I say with pride that never was there a Logan who sought any connection with the stage save in the capacity of a legitimate player.

There were no nude women on the stage in my father's day. Such exhibitions as are now made on the stage of many leading theatres were, in his day, confined to that branch of the show business known as the *Model Artists,* — another perversion of words; but most people know their meaning in their present acceptation.

Across this infamous bridge no Logan ever walked.

And, one by one, every member of our family has left the stage behind, until, at this writing, not one remains upon it; though of their number, there are seven still living who have trod the boards.

Here it is proper that I should.say why I left the stage. The *Commercial Advertiser* and the *Philadelphia Dispatch* are the only journals I have seen which have intimated that my hatred of indecency is born of jealousy; thus implying that I ceased to be an actress because these nude women had encroached upon my territory so far that I was forced to leave, or do what they do.

This is not true. As for the nude women, their reign had not yet set in at the time I left the stage. But I was not forced from the stage at all. My success as an actress was always fully equal to my deserts; and, up to the very day I retired from the stage, I was in receipt of large sums for my services as an actress. As a star (in which capacity I played in the leading theatres of this country, from Wallack's, in New York, to

McVicker's, in Chicago) my earnings were very large, — sometimes reaching one thousand dollars per week. When I played for a salary, the lowest sum I ever received — save when I was a mere child — was one hundred dollars per week.

I left the stage respecting it and many of its people; but my resolve was to live, henceforth, by my pen. I preferred literature to acting, simply on the score of congeniality; and I have never regretted the day when I turned to it. I love it with all my soul, and have several times refused most tempting offers to leave it and return to the stage.

How, then, can I be *jealous* of these women? I am no longer a rival for their place in the theatres. No, it is no such ignoble feeling as this which animates me; it is a feeling of shame that the stage should be so degraded, the drama so disgraced, by the place the nude woman has taken, united to a feeling of sympathy with the numerous modest and virtuous actresses who are crowded from a sphere which they could adorn and honor, — crowded from it *not* by superior talent, nor even by greater beauty, but by sheer brazen immodesty, and by unblushing vice.

I take up next an anonymous letter, dated at Boston, and signed, "A Sister Member of the Profession."

The writer says she is a respectable actress, and professes to be ignorant that gross evils prevail in the theatrical world.

She refers to my letter in the New York *Times*, and asks at what theatre such questions were ever put to an applicant for employment.

In my letter to the *Times*, I said, —

"I referred the other night to decent young women who are not celebrities, — merely honest, modest girls, whose parents have left them the not very desirable heritage of the stage, and who find it difficult to obtain any other employment, being uneducated for any other. When these girls go into a theatre to apply for a situation now, they find that the requirements of managers are expressed in the following questions, —

"1. Is your hair dyed yellow?

"2. Are your legs, arms, and bosom symme-

trically formed, and are you willing to expose
them?

"3. Can you sing brassy songs, and dance the
can-can, and wink at men, and give utterance to
disgusting half words, which mean whole ac-
tions?

"4. Are you acquainted with any rich men
who will throw you flowers, and send you pres-
ents, and keep afloat dubious rumors concerning
your chastity?

"5. Are you willing to appear to-night, and
every night, amid the glare of gas-lights, and
before the gaze of thousands of men, in this pair
of satin breeches, ten inches long, without a ves-
tige of drapery upon your person?

"If you can answer these questions affirma-
tively, we will give you a situation; if not, there's
the door."

At nothing have I been more astonished than
at the manner in which this letter has been received by certain "professionals."

When one of our daily newspapers says that the
streets of this city are in a filthy condition, does
a resident of Fifth Avenue rush down to the

editor's sanctum to call him a liar, and point him to the cleanliness of Fifth Avenue?

It seems incredible that any one could be so stupid as to imagine me making reference to such managers, for. instance, as Edwin Booth, Mr. Field, of the Boston Museum, or Mrs. John Drew, of Philadelphia!

These managers, and a few like them, form the exception to the rule. To such, all honor! But it is a sufficient indication of the enormity of this shame to say that the rage for nudity has intruded in some shape upon the stage of every theatre in this city, *except one.*

Here is a list of the places in this city where the English drama claims, or has claimed, a place, at one time or another, in its highest or its lowest manifestations, —

Academy of Music,	Booth's,
Fisk's Grand Theatre,	Wood's Museum,
Fifth Avenue Theatre,	Theatre Comique,
Wallack's,	The Tammany,
New York Theatre,	The Waverly,
Olympic,	Niblo's Garden,
Broadway Theatre,	Bowery Theatre,
Theatre Français,	Pastor's Opera House.

Two of the above-named places are now closed; but, at this writing, it is rumored that one of them is to be opened for the use of a newly organized troupe of nude women.

Of this whole list, there is but one (Booth's, which is only a few months old) which can claim that it has always been free from any symptom of this licentious fever.

"Four weeks from this time," says the *New York Review* of May 15, "there will be only two theatres in New York that will offer dramatic works. The rest will be show-shops, having as little to do with dramatic art as so many corner groceries."

As to the questions themselves, as printed above, they are, of course, supposititious. It is not said that managers put these exact questions to applicants. It is said that "*the requirements of managers are expressed in these questions.*"

This is strictly true.

It is not necessary, I suppose, to give with the accuracy of a criminal trial report the exact questions which pass between managers and actresses who seek for employment. Their purport

is unmistakable.   Take this one which was
asked a beautiful and modest young woman
whom I have known for years, an actress by profession, who was quietly edged out of her last
situation because she carried decency and
womanly reserve too far in the presence of an
audience which cheered to the echo the nude
creatures who trod the same stage with her, —

 "*Are you up in this style of business ?*"

This question needed no interpreter, — for the
manager pointed, as he spoke, to one of the members of his company, photographed in an immodest attitude, with her legs clad in flesh-colored
silk and her body in a tight-fitting breech-cloth,
richly embroidered.

She was not "up in" this sort of business; she
sought employment as *an actress*; there was none
for her, and she went away, to apply with like
results at other theatres.

She sought employment, as a respectable actress, at fifteen or twenty dollars a week.   She
would have refused five hundred dollars a week
salary to do what the nude woman does.   ·

If the above instance does not indicate mana-

gerial requirements sufficiently, take these statements from managerial lips, —

"Devil take your legitimate drama! I tell
you if I can't draw the crowd otherwise, I'll put
a woman on my stage without a rag on her."

So said a manager of this city in the hearing
of a dozen people; and the disgusting remark
was bandied about from mouth to mouth as if
it had been wit.

A proprietor of one of the theatres above-
named, where a legitimate play was running without paying expenses, rubbed his dry old hands
together, and said, —

" Aha! we must have some of those *fat young
women* in this piece to make it draw."

I go down to Boston for a moment, where
lives this anonymous letter-writing actress who is
so singularly ignorant of what is passing about
her, to mention the rumor which was set afloat
by a manager of a certain one of the blonde
nudities, to the effect that she was once the mistress of the Prince of Wales.

This manager deemed it to his interest to keep

this vile story afloat. It gave an added piquancy to the creature who nightly wriggled about his stage in a dress of silk which fitted her form *all over* as tightly as a glove.

I stay in Boston long enough to note that, in the late Working-woman's Convention there, a lady related the trials of a young friend of hers, who went upon the stage and endured insult and wickedness from managers. The same lady corroborated my own observations, with the statement, that managers look upon the girls they employ as women of the town.

My anonymous " sister member of the profession" has been fortunate beyond most actresses of this period, in coming in contact with nothing of this sort.

I return to New York, to direct attention to that manager of blonde nudities who has won, probably, the most money for his speculations in yellow hair and padded legs of any one in the business.

This person is an Englishman,—said to be, by birth, a gentleman (in the English or aristocratic sense of the word), and who, on entering the theatrical world, concealed his real name.

It is known that this man is a most licentious and shameless *roué*, who publicly boasts of the number of blonde women who have been his mistresses at different times; who actually perpetrated the monstrous indecency of making these infamous boasts in a speech at a dinner where women were present!

Among other things this disgraceful creature said was this: that a certain woman who had broken her professional engagement with him ought to have remembered the fact that she had once been his mistress, and had borne him children!

This infamous boast was coupled with the jeering remark that, in spite of the fact that he had no legal claim upon her services, he had *a moral one* in the fact just stated.

Shame! that such a monster as this should be permitted to remain in this country, the master of a drove of nude women, who are exhibiting themselves nightly to crowded houses, at the largest theatre on Broadway, and fill his already gorged pockets at the expense of disgrace to the dramatic profession, and distress to many of its members!

Were he to be hooted and stoned through the streets of this city, and packed off to England, covered with obloquy, it would be well. But packing him off would hardly rid the stage of this curse, since there are plenty of men besides him who are as vile as he, in all save the infamy of boasting.

With a sigh of relief, I turn to another anonymous letter, dated at New Haven, and signed "One who loves Jesus."

The writer of this letter is evidently a woman. It is tender and sweet in its tone. "I assure you," says the good lady, "your noble stand will be esteemed by all good, moral people." I have abundant proof of that; and if I, in my turn, can lead all such people to think more gently of good and true actors and actresses, I shall thank heaven with a full heart.

"As a child of God," this letter says, "I must esteem the theatre as the devil's play-house."

There was a time, not very long ago, when I should have taken great offence at this. That time is past. I recognize the devil's play-house in the theatre where the nude woman jigs and wriggles.

If there be any such actual entity as that same old theological devil, I can easily imagine him kicking up his hoofs in Mephistophilean joy at the harvests that are falling into his lap from the temples of the nude.

But, dear lady,—you who write me from New Haven,—on the middle ground where I stand, I see what you can not see, and know what you can not know. All theatres do not deserve the stigma of this term. It is true that the theatres which still remain devoted to the drama proper are very, very few; but there are such; and they are no more the " devil's play-house " than is the concert-room where Parepa sings. They are not consecrated to the service of God, it is true; but, at least, they are not given over. to the devil's work.

I respect the theatre in its purity. I respect the actor who is an artist,—even the harmless clown of the pantomime, who makes us laugh without offending decency. That I love so many good and lovely women who are actresses, is my chief reason for deploring the reign of a class of women who are neither good nor lovely, — but coarse, indecent, painted, padded, and dyed.

If it were possible to treat the Nude Woman Question, and leave the nude woman herself out of it, I should be glad to do so. I am the last to wish to give pain to any person; but, in the path of clear duty, there is no choice. When it becomes a question between suffering, struggling virtue, and vice which rolls in luxury, and gathers unto itself wealth by the sheer practice of its wickedness, no woman who loves honor in her sex can hesitate as to the course to be taken.

The spirit of most of the anonymous letters I have received is one which might well cause me to hesitate in the path I have chosen, if fear were stronger in me than principle. But neither the sneers of low-class newspapers, nor the threats of anonymous correspondents, shall have weight with me. I see no other way to effect a cure of this nude woman evil but to make it odious. To that end, I shall do what in me lies. This article is but a beginning. I shall not cease to combat the encroachments of the nude woman upon the domain which should be occupied by true artists, and by virtuous men and women.

Firm in the belief that this indecent army *can* be routed, I call on all honorable souls, both in and out of the profession, to stand by my side and strike hard blows. We shall get hard blows in return, no doubt; but poor indeed must be the panoply of that warrior who can not hold his own against the cohorts of the nude woman. Whatever falls on my head in consequence of my words, I promise to give thrust for thrust. I do not fear the issue.

"Thrice is he armed that hath his quarrel Just.'

XI.

HEN a play is brought out which has a prolonged "run," the world behind the scenes takes on peculiar aspects.

There is a great deal of excitement about it, at first; and pleasurable excitement, too. The reading of the play; the distributing of the "parts"; the rehearsals, although fatiguing, interesting; the suggestions of the author in regard to the making of certain "points"; the desire to succeed,—sometimes, alas! most wofully baffled; the hopes, the fears, the uncertainty,—until, at last, all doubt is set at rest, culminating in the first representation, and then and there ending ignominiously in a failure, or gloriously in "a hit."

A piece which has failed, has fallen, like Luci-

fer, never to rise again. The greatest charity
which can be shown it, is to regard it as a thing
which has never been; or which, having been,
and been badly, can never again be.

Of a thing which has no being, it is obviously
not the duty of a writer to treat; therefore, 'tis
the "crowning success of the season" (whatever it may be), "the talk of the town," the piece
which, in point of fact, has clutched at a single bound the half-dollar diadem of the dress-
circle and displays similar gymnastic tendencies
towards the private boxes and orchestra-stalls,
with which I have now to do.

The nervousness which is so apparent at a first
representation is hardly rubbed off before the
end of the first week. Even if the actor is quite
certain that the remorseless newspaper-man
Scroggins, and the dreaded "dramatic" of the
Weekly *Snarler*, Mr. O'Pinionated, have both
seen it and done their worst or best towards
damning him and the piece, there is still the
fear that others of their class may this night or
never be in "front," and at the very moment
he is debiting his best speech, are engaged

probably in scrawling vindictive phrases against him in the unscrupulous note-book of the critic-mind.

Then, after these persons are disposed of,—when these pen-and-ink skeletons of the dramatic closet are shut up in it and the key turned on them securely,—there presently appears another Bogie as appalling to the actor's mind as to the imagination of the schoolboy the fearful sprites of the Mysteries of Udolpho.

This takes the shape of a rival artist who sits in front and sneers with his lips, his eyes,—sneers with shrugging shoulder and finger-fillip,—sneers with every convenient portion of his anatomy; whispers sneeringly to his next neighbor, laughs sneeringly at the pathetic portion of the play, and looks sneeringly bored at the "jokes." Sneers in every way, and at every thing, until at length the unhappy actor who is being sneered at, losing all heart, soon loses his head,—making forthwith some frightful blunder which really merits sneering from the sneerer and receives its merits to the full.

In spite of this, the poor actor must continue the piece, knowing as well that he will be finally hanged by that military commission of a sneerer in front as any condemned man can know his doom beforehand.

There may be pardon for the most dastardly murderer, at the hands of the governor of the State; but assuredly there is none for the actor, at the hands of his rival (who, by-the-by, invariably comes in on a deadhead ticket).

But after the first eight or ten nights the actor begins to become impervious to all these sights and sounds. No longer troubled about the text, the words come glibly, and ease of action follows as a natural result. This, coupled with the knowledge that the author has given him a cheering word, or the manager, perhaps, expressed satisfaction with his efforts, inspires him with new courage, and, for the nonce, he plays the part,—not so well as it might be played, doubtless,—but certainly as well as he can play it.

This would be a very desirable state of things, if it could continue. But in this wicked world of ours what thing can continue, or what state of things can continue at the neutral point of being simply satisfactory?

14

Soon the actor begins to tire of his part. The speeches, which, during the first few weeks of the run of the piece, he gave with such *élan*, — the jokes which he then uttered with such mirth and *intention*, — have now become, whatever they may be to the audience, an old story to the actor.

He wonders how they can laugh at the witticisms which, to his mind, are stale, or applaud the heroics now to him so very flat and unprofitable.

Between his "waits" he falls as nearly asleep as he dares, and goes on the stage fully as dull as he can.

He is astonished that such crowds will still flock to see the piece. For himself he is "sick" of it, and yet dreads the trouble which the "getting-up" of another would involve.

So, divided between actual discontent with this, and anticipated discontent of the other, he goes on in that dramatic treadmill widely known as the "run of a piece."

Sometimes he has good reason to be weary. Sometimes a little melo-drama without music, or

a tragedy not written in blank verse, has been en-
acted around his own hearthstone, with his wife
and children in the principal parts. Mariana,
his bride, has died, perhaps, before the end of the
fifth act; or his children have been strangled, not
like the young Princes, in a dungeon at the
tower, but in his own poor room, spite of all
efforts to save them, by the murderous hand of
the destroyer—Diphtheria.

Never mind. Take up thy staff, Jew, and
wander on through the intricate mazes of the
"run" of a piece.

I have had experience in this sort myself, more
than once. I mind me of a particular night
when I was playing my last engagement on
the stage,—at the Broadway theatre, now, like
myself, no longer part of the mimic world.

As I was going on the stage, I heard of the
death of a man whom I had scarcely seen above
a dozen times in my life,— whom, if he had lived,
I might not have met another dozen times in
as many years,—yet whom I grieved for as for a
dead brother, for he was of the brotherhood of
those who love the good, the unsullied, the true,

the truly beautiful, and spoke his love in poesy which still echoes down the avenues of time.

Do you wonder that the wit of the author of our piece suffered at my hands that night? That his repartee I made pointless, and his sentiment not less so?

The trained lips smiled, and the false laugh rang out merrily as before; but instead of the crowd of pleasure-seekers who had come to see our comedy that night, my dimmed eyes kept conjuring up and gazing sadly, tenderly, upon a beautiful dead face which so short a time ago sparkled in its every feature with the brilliancy of the beautiful mind behind it.

"Ah, well," I sighed, "the turf will rest lightly on that brave young breast; flowers will spring spontaneously on the sod which covers that poetic heart,—more fresh, more lovely, more tender than the fragrantest flowers themselves!"

We all feel and know that heaven is a beautiful place, and we are all trying, in different ways and each after his own fashion, to get there.

But this will never do, will it ?

You engaged me for your light-comedy business, and here I am sitting with tears falling on the paper fast as rain, and experiencing the most undeniable want of a pocket-handkerchief !

I don't wear spectacles yet, and therefore can not lose them ; but handkerchiefs have a peculiar way of wandering from my gaze like a beautiful dream, and my only resource being to get up and seek fresh ones, limits my stock very soon, and awakens recrimination in the breast of the washerwoman, who has plainly avowed to me that henceforth and forever two handkerchiefs shall count as two pieces, and not (as heretofore) as one.

This arithmetic of the laundry, which goes to prove the somewhat paradoxical fact that one and one make one, is perhaps a novelty to you.

I hope it is so.

It proves that your shirt-bosom's lord sits lightly on his throne.

But I assure you that this singular multiplication-table is practised, like accidents, in the best-regulated families.

14 *

From handkerchiefs I return, Othello-like, to the theatre.

A cheerful feature in the "run" of a piece is the weekly matinée, which style of performance is now very popular, and patronized almost exclusively by the sweetest beings who can patronize a theatre, — sweet women and sweeter children.

The dear little Latter stare at the play with all their eyes, and clap their little chubby hands, and show other unmistakable signs of glee, until at last they get tired, and sleepy, and fretful, and have to be taken home.

The dear Former, little and great, stout and slender, young and old, laugh with the children, — interfere with the players a little by explaining the plot of the piece in concise and baby language, and point one of them out as the lady who was at grandma's to tea the other evening, which fact baby declines to believe, on the ground that she wore a black silk dress then, and is differently costumed now; and presently the curtain comes down for good, leaving the question still unsettled and still in dispute.

Sweet, sweet little credulous children! Bright,

pretty young wives and mothers! It is worth acting at a matinée, if for nought else than to see the charming sight which together you present.

But for all that, it is dull work.

Especially if it happens to be a rainy day, when everything without is dark, and wretched, and gloomy.

Especially if it happens to be a sunshiny day, when everything without is glad, and glorious and free, and when the wretchedness, and gloom, and darkness are within, — sometimes, alas! hid away in the depths of our bleeding, throbbing hearts.

A ray of sunlight striking through the chink of an ill-closed door, overpowers the gas and shows the hideousness of a painted face by daylight. Shows the falsity of all things. The pasteboard goblets; the unsteady thrones which look inviting enough to the eye but which prove treacherous as real ones do, when you try to mount their steps. Shows the spider's web, and the unguarded fly left to pursue its destiny alone. Shows that the royal purple is very cheap stuff, indeed. Shows that much that glitters is not gold.   Shows that there is no ink in the inkstand, and that the quill-pen has no point.   Shows the marriage contract blank to this day though it has been used fifty times, and ostensibly signed and sealed.

And I muse on the hollowness and emptiness of things, — for it is not on the stage alone that things are not what they seem.

My thoughts wander back through the story of an eventful life, full of strange vicissitudes; and presently find myself far away from the mimic world, in fancy again viewing the realties of that glittering period, — my first year in Paris.

XII.

ABOUT MY FIRST YEAR IN PARIS.

Y position was a peculiar one in many respects, when I was in my seventeenth year of life on earth, my first year of life in Paris.

My daily companions were the ladies and gentlemen of Louis Napoleon's court. It was erroneously believed that to get admitted to the *salons* where I presided, was equivalent to setting foot in the very ante-room of royalty, — a belief, the existence of which, I must in justice say, was at the time unknown to me, and for which I was in no way responsible.

I now had my first taste of the power of Power, — or, more properly speaking, of the power of *supposed* Power. There were all sorts of people at my doors incessantly, wanting all

sorts of favors, — from the sale to the French
government of a patent valued at a million
francs, to the securing of a seat in the imperial
chapel at the Tuileries for the coming Sunday
morning, — and as I was at that age when one
wishes to please everybody, I always did my
little best to get everybody's requests granted.

There were French people, and English people,
and people of all lands, among these haunters of
my threshold, but more than all others, there
were Americans.

The generality of these, like true-born Yankees as they were, had "inventions" which they
were anxious to sell to the government. Gene-
ally, it was something in the way of fire-arms,
though sewing-machines, bread-making machines,
and many other machines, found their way to
,my residence in the Faubourg St. Honoré for
inspection.

To find an *American* — these deluded people
thought — in such a very exceptional position,
was something most extraordinary: a person who
could look at your inventions in one minute, and

twenty minutes later stand in the emperor's presence and speak directly to him about them, — it was wonderful! Such a person *must* be got at, — must be propitiated, and made to take a personal interest in every inventor's cause.

It was not difficult to say a good word for these worthy men. Generally, however, the inventions were chimerical illusions, or delusions, whose uselessness it only required a practical test to clearly demonstrate.

One of these, I well remember, was a bread-baking apparatus, presented by a gentleman of Cincinnati, whose cause I espoused with especial enthusiasm in view of his hailing from the western city where my mother, brother, and sisters lived. To hear of the operations of this wonderful apparatus was like listening to a fairy story, or to a modern rivalry of the miracle of the loaves and fishes.

For this inventor permission was obtained to land his apparatus in Havre, free of duty; and there the matter ended, because the machine stopped working in America, and refused ever to resume its marvelous operations.

One of the Yankees, though not one of the impecunious, was Mr. Cyrus W. Field. He spent much time at my house, in his efforts to secure a concession from the French government of the right to land a submarine cable on the French islands of St. Pierre and Miquelon.

My interest in this matter was very strong. While it was still pending, I left Paris for a few weeks' sojourn at Biarritz, the imperial sea-bathing village. M. Mocquard was there with the empress, and I wrote to him on the subject, urging him, if possible, to let me have the concession for Mr. Field at once.

Mocquard's position as Napoleon's right-hand man, his mouthpiece, his confidential adviser, was well known. To apply to him was as good as, or better than, to apply to the emperor himself.

With his never-failing courtesy, Mocquard expressed to me his regret at not being able to respond to my desire. He wrote, —

" I must, before writing to Paris, confer about this matter with the Minister of Foreign Affairs, now at Biarritz. Repose in me the care of giving it an active impulsion. Believe in my affectionate sentiments.

" Mocquard."

I had frequent opportunities of observing the peculiar nervousness of Mr. Field's temperament, superinduced, no doubt, by his exciting labors.

I remember one day when we were driving about from one *Ministère* to another, receiving disheartening answers from all (for people were then disposed to look upon the whole business as a chimera, and on its projector as an amiable lunatic), how amused I was with Mr. Field's eccentricity.

While discussing the glories of his pet scheme with great volubility in English, he would repeatedly interrupt himself to punch the astonished driver in the back, and ejaculate the one word *Allez* — " go on ! "

The man was already racing his horses at their

15

full speed, but Mr. Field's eagerness far out-stripped their shodden heels.

The style of the utterance was somewhat this:

" I tell you it is not a mad idea." [Punch—*Allez !*]   " The day is not far distant when you will see the two countries joined." [Punch—*Allez !*]   " Just think of it ! Instantaneous communication between London and New York!" [Punch—*Allez !*]

The scene was brought to a farcical climax when the driver, impatient at last beyond endurance, turned around in his seat and mumbled in that tone of suppressed rage common to the French and English subordinate when angry,—

"*Ah ça ! vous m'embetez à la fin !*"—" Come now ! you pester me, at last ! "

This mild protest against the punches and the reiterated *allez*, Mr. Field did not take the pains to notice, if he even understood.

When he was just on the point of receiving the concession, Mr. Field discovered that a mistake had been made in a date,—purposely, as it afterward appeared.

" The date is wrong," said honest Mr. Field.

"I can not sign a petition which states that I shall be in Paris on that date."

"I know that you will be gone, Monsieur," said the official, blandly, "but as a matter of form it was necessary that the date should be thus."

"But I shall be on the ocean at that time," said Mr. Field.

"Where you will," rejoined the official, shrugging his shoulders. "It does not matter. Sign, all the same."

"No," said the American gentleman, with noble simplicity, "I· can not sign. Who knows but I may be lost at sea on this trip? In that case I could not bear the thought that almost my last act in Europe was to indorse a falsehood."

The concession was obtained at last, however, and Mr. Field proved the feasibility of his scheme.

Among the numerous applicants for another kind of favor—the obtaining of a contract—was a person who now "enjoys" a somewhat unenviable reputation from having had a price set on his head by the American government just after the death of Lincoln. I allude to Mr. Beverly Tucker, whose term of office as United States Consul at Liverpool had just expired, and who was now in Paris for the purpose of working what he joyously but erroneously quoted as his "gold mine."

In other words, he hoped 'to obtain a contract for supplying beef to that portion of the French army then operating in China.

A circumstance here unnecessary to relate led the voluble Southerner to implore my assistance in the matter. In a weak moment I consented, and writing to M. Mocquard obtained a letter of audience for myself and (alas, for French ignorance of a patronymic so distinguished!) for my *pro tem.* protégé, M. BEWERLY TUKE!

To make my folly complete I had consented to act on this occasion in the somewhat undignified capacity of interpreter, as Mr. Tucker was unable to master more than half a dozen words of French.

On the day appointed for the audience we drove to the Tuileries, and were admitted to the presence of the *Chef du Cabinet.*

I could not have conceived it possible that a man of Beverly Tucker's years, — one who had so recently held a somewhat important post in England, a person of considerable consequence, no doubt, in the South, — would be so completely overthrown by the august presence of M. Mocquard.

Royalty itself never should have abashed an American gentleman thus; and Mocquard, important as he was, was not royalty at least.

Tucker's self-possession immediately deserted him, and during the entire interview he never once recovered it. Naturally of a florid complexion, with sandy hair and fiery red beard, his tinge now deepened into a gorgeous scarlet. I was almost frightened myself when I looked at him, — not that I was awed by Mocquard, but that I feared Tucker would presently fall into an apoplectic fit.

Mocquard's cabinet was immediately contiguous to that of the emperor, on the ground floor

15 *

of the Palace of the Tuileries, looking out upon the English Garden which the emperor had recently cut off from the public inclosure for the exclusive use of the imperial family, — an act, by-the-way, much to the annoyance of the Parisians, who looked upon the Tuileries, every square foot of it, as the natural play-ground of the children of France, the rendezvous of the becapped *bonne* with her soldier-spark, the home of the coco-vendor, the land of the *marchande de plaisirs.*

Gazing out upon the floral beauties which smiled thus at our feet, staring amazedly at the antique glories of upholstery and fresco which the room afforded, my companion, for the first time in my acquaintance with him, became thoroughly oblivious of his "gold mine," and of the presence of the person whose capital of influence — not money — was to work the treasure.

It was not until I recalled him to a sense of where he was, by repeatedly pronouncing the secretary's name, that he became conscious of the great breach of etiquette he was committing by his *gauche* and oblivious manner.

Then began the embarrassment and the redness; and on the part of the secretary an impatience and dislike of this beefy-looking man whom he evidently considered a boor, which showed me I had a delicate part to play.

The matter of the "gold mine" explained, M. Mocquard answered that it was something which did not come within his province, and that all he could do for Mr. Tucker was to give him letters of introduction to the head officials of those *Ministères* who "occupied themselves" with contracts and shipments of stores.

This in itself was a great favor, and when I explained it to Mr. Tucker he was so very grateful for it that he took upon himself to use four out of the six French words he knew.

They were these, dropped slowly, and with dire emphasis on the last one, —

"*Je—remercie—votre—excellence*"—(I—thank — your — excellency).

Here was a bit of insolent ignorance!

Mocquard, the life-long friend of the emperor,—the last and best-beloved lover of his mother, Queen Hortense,—the pet of the empress — Commander in the order of the Legion of Honor, — *chef* of the cabinet, — to whom the emperor had offered every title from duke to baron, and who had refused all to retain the simple, illustrious, and, as he thought, world-known name of Mocquard, — to be addressed by the *banal* and mediocre title of " excellency," by an unpleasant American with ill manners and a red face!

It was like a slur thrown on the device of the Rohans.

Roy ne puis.	King, I can not.
Prince ne daigne.	Prince, I deign not.
Rohan, je suis!	Rohan, I am!

Again came the fatal phrase, "*Je — remercie — votre — excellence.*"

" Tell him I am no ' excellency!'" said the indignant Mocquard to me, haughtily rising to put an end to the interview.

Alas! Tucker heeded not, and again, —

"*Je — remercie —*"

"*Diable!*" ejaculated Mocquard, stamping his foot; " he pesters me! "

I edged my unfortunate compatriot out of the presence as expeditiously as possible, and when we were again in the carriage, I asked Mr. Tucker why he had not taken my hint, at the same time explaining how very annoying it was to Mocquard to be called "excellency."

"Oh, sho!" said this perfectly self-complacent son of the sunny South, "that's all gammon! He liked it, never tell me! They all like it. I tell you it *tickles* 'em to be called excellencies, these Frenchmen."

I explained the peculiar nature of this case, but to no purpose. The obtuseness of this really kind-hearted but stupid "chivalrous" person was very amusing.

Our first visit, after leaving Mocquard, was to the Ministry of the Marine, where a polite but imperative "impossible," from the lips of M. Dupuy de Lome effectually closed up Mr. Beverly Tucker's "gold mine," which was never heard of more.

But it is not alone the Yankee inventor or would-be contractor who comes before the throne of Louis Napoleon. American authors and publishers are also much in the habit of courting imperial notice.

To what an extent this is done, few people in this country are aware; because, as a rule, with most rare exceptions, these efforts to obtain notice from Napoleon or Eugénie fail utterly of accomplishing any thing.

Once in a while an American author or publisher gets a letter of praise or a present of jewelry; but even in that case it by no means follows that the work is really valued by the emperor or empress. The letter or the present may be a whim, or it may be a piece of policy.

I recall the case of a well-known publisher who sent the emperor the most beautiful specimen of the bookmaker's art on which my eyes ever feasted, — a Worcester's Dictionary, printed on satin paper, soft as a baby's cheek, bound gorgeously in green morocco decked with gold, with the imperial arms and cipher dextrously inserted at every available point, gilt-edged, perfumed, — a very triumph in its way.

Arrived at the palace, this book carelessly

knocked about from one room to another, cared
for by nobody ; until, feeling sorry for it as if it
were a living thing, I one day asked why it was
so ill-treated.

"*Ah, Diable!*" said M. Mocquard, impatiently,
"these things pester us. I, for one, wish people
would stop sending them. If you want it, you
can have it."

"But will not the emperor object to my having taken it?"

"*Parbleu!*" said the secretary, shrugging his
shoulders, and laughing with a manner half droll,
half contemptuous, "what does the Emperor of
France care for *Woochestaire Sauce's Diction-
aire!*"

This case is not related because there is any
thing out of the common in it. Quite the contrary. It chanced to be the first of several
elegant books which were freely given to me,
which came to the Tuileries in the same way.

Nearly all of these were from American authors or publishers, though a few were from
English sources, and, it is easy to conceive, were
the centre of many a fond hope, and prepared

at great expense of time, labor, and money, for their special purpose.

How little those who devised them imagined that their carefully prepared gifts would find no better fate than that of being given again to his friends by the amiable Mocquard!

XIII.

ABOUT MOCQUARD.

OR ten years or more, Jean Mocquard wrote nearly every word that was spoken from the throne of Louis Napoleon, and penned every official document which issued from that cabinet on which the eyes of Europe were centered.

Vehemently as the emperor would no doubt deny such an assertion, it is very nearly certain that by far the greater portion of *La Vie de César* was indited by the veinous hand of the old French lawyer, Mocquard.

Writing was his passion, — at once his labor and his relaxation.

My first acquaintance with him was in the year 1857. He was then very busy writing his novel " Jessie," and, like many other even more

16

illustrious authors, he was glad enough to obtain an "idea" from any source, however humble. For this reason it was no extraordinary thing for him to solicit an interview with me, from time to time, for the purpose of reading what he had written, obtaining my judgment on it, and then questioning me in regard to what I considered the most natural sequence to the story as it ran. Perhaps this was an undue honor for "one of my age"; but the secret of it no doubt lay in Mocquard's opinion that my knowledge of dramatic effect might prove of advantage to one who, like himself, was seeking the play-wright's honors as well as those of the novelist.

"Tell me all about the American theatre," he would say; "make me to know some details of the Yankee *camaraderie.*"

His novel "Jessie," which had a most extraordinary sale, was founded in part upon incidents which I related to him as having occurred in the history of my sister.

The reader of "Jessie" will remember the episode of the Southern planter, who, in love with the actress, sends her as a present, two negro slaves.

Jessie replies to this wooer (who tells her that the bondmen are not so fettered as he) to this effect:

"I accept your gift only to bestow freedom on your serfs. They shall have their liberty, — keep yours."

I well remember the enthusiasm with which Mocquard received this bit of childish reminiscence. How he clapped his hands together, exclaiming, —

"And this was your sister? You may be proud, *oui!* She aided the cause of liberty, *pardieu!* Jessie shall do as much."

"Jessie" was translated into every modern language, selling by thousands of copies in every civilized country of the world.

There can be no doubt that this success was due less to the merits of the book than to the exalted position of the author. Every body wanted to read a work written by the chief of the emperor's cabinet.

Mocquard ignored this fact completely, and believed that the wonderful sale of the novel was entirely due to its merits, which he frankly confessed to me he considered as *hors ligne.*

Although my own opinion of this particular work was scarcely so flattering, Mocquard's high literary ability was unquestionable. This ability was best displayed in his plays.

The best known of these is one which had an immensely long "run," though the subject is that threadbare one, now, alas! no longer peculiar to French literature, which is sufficiently indicated by the title of the play, *"La Fausse Adultère."*

Another of Mocquard's plays, *"La Tireuse de Cartes,"* is known to the American public as " Gamea, the Jewish Mother," another translation of it being dubbed " The Woman in Red." This play was written at the time of the abduction of the Jewish child Mortara, and has that incident as a plot.

Still another, a garbled translated version of which was played by Miss Bateman, and called " Rosa Gregorio," was *"Les Fiancés d'Albano."*

In this play a direct appeal was made to the chivalrous sentiments of honor of the French. It was brought out very soon after the attempted assassination of the emperor, as he was entering

the opera-house, and in it an actor was made to
utter these words to a murderer,—

" Begone ! you are a coward,—*for an assassin
is always a coward.*"

A line which " brought down the house" very
successfully, particularly on the night of the
first representation, when the emperor and empress were present. Both Napoleon and Eugénie bowed in response to the hearty cheering,
which had but one signification,— abhorrence
of the attempted crime and satisfaction at its
failure.

Mocquard's name was not given as the author
of these plays.

The Drama is a powerful lever with which
to move the mass; and when some pet bit of
policy was entertained by the imperial cabinet,
Mocquard produced a play in which the same
appeared, " tried it on" the people, and if it was
favorably received, adopted it.

Americans would think it rather strange, if, before purchasing Russian America, the Executive
at Washington had caused such an incident to be
inserted in a play for the purpose of seeing how

16 *

it worked with the mass; but it would seem that in some things a democratic government dares be more despotic than despotism itself.

It was, therefore, wholly for state reasons that Mocquard denied himself the satisfaction of hearing his name announced on "first nights" as author of the piece "which we have had the honor of presenting before you," and transferred all the glory and part of the money to Monsieur Victor Sejour, a professional dramatist, who was undoubtedly Mocquard's skillful *collaborateur.*

Mocquard's mode of composition was very curious. If an idea struck him at any moment he would stop all else to note it down. He has told me that it frequently happened to him to make the emperor wait for state business while he was jotting down ideas for his next new play, or devising some touching love-situation for "Jessie."

On one occasion I saw him stop eating his noonday breakfast, and, with his mouth full of chicken, rush over to his writing-table, seize a quill, and hurriedly pen-photograph some brilliant thought; then, throwing back his head, and striking a tragic attitude, with the drumstick of the chicken in one hand and the manuscript in the other, he declaimed it aloud and cried out to me, —

"*Eh bien, eh bien!* what do you think of *that ?* That's Tacitus, isn't it ? "

Tacitus was to him the great model.

Mocquard derived a considerable income from his plays, and made a sum which was no bagatelle out of his percentage on the sales of " Jessie."

In person this astute Frenchman was of medium height, and of excessive leanness both of face and figure. IIis hair was scant and gray, but to the day of his death his eye retained its wonderful brightness and his speech its fluent grace.

IIe was excessively fond of fast horses, and one of his favorite amusements was to indulge in private races with those of his friends who had " some *trotteurs,*" as he expressed it, which could compete with his own.

* IIe frequently begged me to come to the Bois de Boulogne to witness such friendly matches

between himself and Mr. Charles Astor Bristed, but as they were appointed for an unpleasantly early hour in the morning I was obliged to decline.

Mocquard had three children, — one a lawyer of no particular eminence, who is still practising in Paris; the second, an officer in a regiment of *Spahis*, stationed in Algeria; and a daughter married into an immensely wealthy *roturière* family, the wife of Mr. Raimbault, a gentleman who distinguished himself in the summer of 1867 by saving the life of the Czar by striking a pistol from the hands of the Pole who attempted to assassinate the imperial Russian.

Mocquard's salary was nominally only five thousand dollars a year; but that he had other sources of income is evident from the fact that he left a fortune of many millions of francs.

He occupied a magnificent *suite* of parlors in the Rue de Rivoli; directly opposite the Palace of the Tuileries, during the winter months; and when the court was at St. Cloud, a charming cottage in the park of Montretout was provided for this adviser of the emperor. At the palaces of Compiègne and Fontainebleau, and at the imperial villas at Plombières and Biarritz, he had rooms adjoining those of his majesty.

In early years he must have been a very attractive man, and even at the age of seventy his wit was fresher and more sparkling than that of any Frenchman I ever met, which is saying much among a nation of *beaux esprits.*

It was well known in France that he had been the last lover of the Queen Hortense, the mother of the present emperor; and this fact, singularly enough, was his chief claim for favor with Napoleon the Third, who, to show his gratitude, created him a commander in the Legion of Honor, appointed him chief of the imperial cabinet, as well as private secretary to the emperor, and offered him any title he might choose from the long list beginning at Prince and ending at Vicomte. Titles, however, Mocquard declined.

One day, when I was strolling with him in the private park of the palace at St. Cloud, he stopped suddenly, and, laying his hand on my arm, said, with a gravity which was not usual with him,—

"*Mon enfant*, if you were to rack your brain forever to find subjects for romances, you could invent *nothing* so marvellous as my life. I have suffered privation in every shape,—hunger, thirst, and even the want of a bed; and now look at me," and he drew himself up proudly while I did so, "I am one of the leading diplomatists in Europe, and the friend of un EMPEREUR!"

He swelled his voice proudly on the glorious title, and shook his gaunt finger, stretched at arm's-length above his head, in a most impressive though somewhat theatrical manner.

Having thus set me to thinking on the strange vicissitudes and triumphs which it is the fate of some of us to encounter, he suddenly, to my intense surprise, burst out into a species of Mephistophelean laughter, and twisting his body as though his great mirth was thus distorting it, he whispered, hoarsely,—

"We concoct deviltries enough, he and I."

"He" was the Emperor Napoleon.

I think this confession was a bubbling over of the "deviltries," and almost inadvertently made; but that it was true seems probable enough when coupled with the fact that half an hour after the death of Mocquard the emperor caused seals to be placed on all his private secretary's papers, that no one, not even his own children, should read the history of the "deviltries" until the imperial hand had put them into angelic shape.

XIV.

ABOUT HOME LIFE IN PARIS.

THE home life of Paris is a thing with which few Americans ever become ·acquainted.

The ordinary tourist, who rushes about from one continental city to another, in the headlong manner for which Americans are celebrated, returns to his native land with no more idea of the interior life of the Parisian than he would have if he had never been abroad.

Indeed, he not unfrequently jumps to the conclusion that there is no home life in Paris at all.

He sees so many people out-doors so continually, — sitting on the iron chairs, reading, in the Champs Elysées, and on the Boulevards, and everywhere, — thronging the streets, gayly attired, and so evidently bent on pleasure, recrea-

tion, not business, — so many ladies, so many children, so many servants, — a never-intermitting
crowd of strollers and gazers, unmistakably
French, — that it is no wonder he concludes the
people of Paris live out of doors, take their meals
at restaurants, and only go under a roof at bed-
time.

It is true that the French have a never-falter-
ing faith in the beneficence of the open air. In
pleasant weather, no French mother permits her
children to remain in-doors.

Out-doors is the place for children, say the
Parisians; and out they go, early in the morning,
accompanied by nurse, and out they stay till the
daylight is done, and the darkness falls (or as
much darkness as ever falls on the brightly-lighted
streets of Paris); only coming in at meal-times
for a brief *séance* about the family-board.

It is true that the Parisian believes there is
champagne in the air, and goes out whenever he
can to quaff it.

But there are homes in Paris, and in those
homes families bound together by ties as firm as
those which hold kith and kin in any land.

Parisian houses are, in great part, built of a light cream-colored stone, which is soft when it comes from the quarry, and is carved and fashioned by the sculptor-stonemason into a thousand beautiful and fantastic shapes, which harden and live by the action of the air.

The man who carves those fine heads which we see ornamenting the cornices of windows in Paris buildings, — who fashions the magnificent caryatides who seem to bear on their brawny shoulders the weight of the whole structure, — is no mean artisan.

In France, any boy who desires to be a sculptor is furnished the instruction of the best masters, free of charge. After a certain time has elapsed, if he shows extraordinary talent, he is sent by the country to Rome. If, on the other hand, it appears on trial that he has not genius enough to be a sculptor in the highest sense of the word, he then falls back upon the broad field of sculptor of stone for the fronts of houses.

The stone is carved after the house is built, — not before, as one would suppose.

Paris houses generally range in height from six

stories to nine. The ground-floor of a French house is devoted to the carriage-way, for entrance into the court-yard. This yard is at the back, and around it are ranged the stables, coach-houses, etc.

On the ground-floor is also situated the apartment of the concierge, — a sort of janitor, in a larger sense. This person receives all letters for the dwellers in the house; instructs callers which way to go, and how many flights of stairs there are to mount; attends to the letting of vacant apartments, and is also the most valuable aid in Paris to the police, — furnishing that body with every information in regard to the ladies and gentlemen abiding in the house.

It is easy to see that the ladies and gentlemen aforesaid are very much at the mercy of these concierges.

The result is, that they are profusely feed by all; for if they be not conciliated, they can cause one a deal of annoyance in the way of keeping back letters, cards, etc., to say nothing of graver troubles in connection with the police, whose spies they are.

The "first floor" of the French is after the first flight of stairs — not on the ground, as with us. This the French call the *première étage*. It is naturally the most expensive in the house.

In Paris houses, looking-glasses are furnished the lodger; and in every apartment, however small, as many as two, and often three elegant mirrors will invariably be found. So also with chandeliers.

Of course, I am speaking now of unfurnished rooms.

Gas is little used *chez soi* in Paris. The French do not like it. They urge a thousand objections to it.

It smokes the furniture, it injures pictures, it · kills plants (of which the French are very fond, always having a number growing in their rooms), and lastly (and most important), feminine beauty is sorely tried by its glaring, *discovering* light, while it is delightfully softened and enhanced by the mellow gleam of waxen tapers.

The second story is always less expensive than the first, and the rents go on diminishing as they reach the top.

It is no extraordinary thing to find people of poverty, almost verging on starvation, occupying the topmost floor of a house on whose lower floors dwell millionnaires and titled people.

Generally, however, these poor apartments are reached by a separate staircase, which is also devoted to the uses of the servants of the great personages, and further serves as a mode of ingress and egress for such necessary creatures as the butcher, the baker, the charcoal-man, and the water-man.

Though I consider Paris as peculiarly the City of Luxury, there is one great luxury (none the less luxurious because it is a necessity) in which the smallest American town is more luxurious than Paris. This is water. Water is scarce At Home, in Paris.

I have heard it said that wine is cheaper than water there; but that is a pleasant fiction.

Water is brought to Paris homes every morning by men who sell it at two sous a pail. The water-cooler is filled for a certain sum. This is only water to drink, and to use in cooking; a

17 *

hydrant in the yard furnishes water in limited quantities for lavatory purposes.

If one wants a bath, application may be made at a bath-house near by.

For three francs (sixty sous) a bath-tub will be brought, set down in your bed-room, filled with hot or cold water, into which perhaps a bag of bran has been thrown (a favorite emollient for the skin with the French) and your bath is ready. But besides this a heater is brought, filled with hot and clean towels in abundance.

Three francs pays for all, as well as for the removal of the bath, etc., at the time you specify.

Of course, if you choose to go to one of the public bath-houses (in which Paris abounds) all this may be had much cheaper.

The system of household management in Paris would no doubt astonish many American ladies.

No "lady," no "gentleman," can go to market. The market-place is altogether the resort of the lower orders.

So long as an effort is made to appear genteel

—no matter on how poor a scale—a servant must be sent to the market.

This is the servant's legitimate field for swindling. No policeman can follow her here. If she pays fifty sous for a pair of chickens, and chooses to put down on her account-book that she paid seventy-five sous for them, it is no easy matter to find out the truth.

If you were even to so far forget your "lady"-hood as to go to the market-woman and inquire, she would vow, with shrieks to yourself and *le bon Dieu* to believe her, that the servant-woman paid exactly what she said she had.

The explanation is simple. Generally, the market-woman has sympathy for the woman of her class; with that fierce rage of the French lower orders, she hates you for being her superior, and is glad your servant can cheat you. But particularly, your cook has been her customer for years,—will be, in all probability, for years to come. If you choose to come to the market and buy for yourself, she and all the other market-women will form a league against you, and cheat you worse than the cook does.

This is one of the things that make marketing
in Paris unduly expensive.

Another thing which makes it so, is, that,
store-room being almost an impossibility, it is
difficult to buy anything by the quantity, as flour
or sugar by the barrel, butter by the firkin, etc.
These necessaries must be bought by driblets, at
an unduly exorbitant price, to which is added the
illegitimate percentage of the cook.

Another curious custom with the French is in
the mode of engaging servants.

No Frenchwoman of the proper sort will be
satisfied with a written recommendation from a
servant; such are too easily procured to be relia-
ble: she must see the servant's last mistress, and
make of her every imaginable inquiry.

Thus it is that people who are as far apart in
the social system as Herschel is from the Sun in
the astronomical, are swept together by the incon-
trovertible law of custom every time a servant is
changed.

Canaille may call on Duchess; yes, and, what
is more, question that duchess, pin her in a corner,
ask her if she is quite certain she is telling the

truth about her ex-servant; and Duchess will and must — without loss of temper — answer every question.

If she be not altogether too fashionable a duchess she will call, in her turn, when she wants a servant, and ask Canaille if the reasons why they separated were derogatory to the servant's character.

A curious type of French servitor in Paris homes is the *frotteur*, or floor-rubber.

Carpets are frequently altogether dispensed with in French homes; though the rich people indulge in them, it is as in any other luxury.

That a carpet should be a *necessity*, is to the French a ridiculous bit of New-World nonsense.

Even the rich dispense with them in dining-rooms; and the well-rubbed, shining oaken floors make a very pretty appearance.

The *frotteur* charges a franc or two an hour for his labor, furnishing his own wax, with a great yellow lump of which he proceeds to rub the floor, as a woman might do with a bit of soap preparatory to scrubbing it.

Then, like her in some degree again, he takes a dry scrubbing-brush with a leathern strap across the top, and (unlike her now), inserting his *foot* in the loop, begins rubbing away lustily, singing like a good fellow the while, and using his disengaged foot for the purpose of preserving his equilibrium. When one leg is tired, he alternates ; and so to the end.

When the floor shines like a mirror, and the *frotteur's* face likewise, you will hear his voice at your bedroom-door, singing out, in jolly numbers, —

" Madame, will she have the *obligeance* to pay her good *frotteur*, if you please ? "

Many ladies, who keep no man-servant, and who shrink from the expense of a *frotteur* (for the French are very economical), exact that the floor-rubbing shall be done by the maid-servant. But this is generally objected to by the poor little grisettes.

The very first question they ask before entering a new service, is, " Is your maid expected to do the floor-rubbing ? " They say physicians tell them it is bad exercise for women ; and no doubt it is.

The Movement-Cure advocates will be glad to learn that it is said the legs of the *frotteurs*, developed by this curious work, are perfect in form, and that these honest fellows are in demand as models by the artists.

So floor-rubbing is good for something, — besides the floors.

It is certainly very bad for the carpet-trade.

Charcoal is altogether used for cooking purposes in France; and wood is used to heat the apartments, to the almost entire exclusion of coal, which the Parisians hold in abhorrence.

They contend that coal ruins furniture, spoils one's complexion, and chokes up the lungs with its gritty particles.

I have in vain represented to French people that the Americans were a healthy race, though they burned coal, as a rule, in their cities; and that the great wood-fires of the French, in their old-fashioned fireplaces with andirons, though very poetic, and very cheerful to look at, give out a wofully poor heat for the money.

To those Americans who have never been to Paris, it may no doubt seem a curious thing that rich people should live together in what we call, even at its best, a tenement-house, — that is to say, on separate floors.

Nevertheless, the system is an excellent one, and far preferable to the life in hotels and boarding-houses, which is so common in this country in the large cities.

A parlor, a dining-room, four or five bedrooms, a kitchen, and servant's room may easily be obtained in Paris at almost any rent desired — subject, of course, to such considerations as the elegance of the *appartement*, the location of the house, and the location of the suite of rooms *in* the house.

The floors are complete in all their appointments; and thus the strictest privacy is insured.

Indeed, so free are the Parisians from the prying eyes of their co-lodgers, that it is possible to live twenty years in a house and never meet a single occupant of it, except, perhaps, on the staircase (common ground), where a slight bow passes, — even between utter strangers.

For my own part, I sincerely wish the prejudice, in our country, against these houses could be removed, and that the abominable system of boarding-houses might be broken up, — a system which is directly conducive to idle habits, gossiping, and other evils, even greater.

In Paris, only a few, a very few families, occupy houses to themselves. Those who do, live for the most part in the Faubourg Saint-Germain, the quarter aristocratic *par excellence* of the gay city.

These are the noble families who look upon the present emperor as a vile *parvenu*, and pray that the day may not be long deferred when the perfumed and spotless Bourbon lily shall chase from sovereign banners the buzzing and stinging bee of the Bonapartes.

Still, in the modern and more bustling parts of the town, some grand private houses may be seen, — even outstripping in grandeur, and in gilding, and in glittering newness, the solemn and severe old homes of France's "fine flower" of nobility. These lie along the avenue of the Champs Elysées, the boulevard de l'Impératrice,

18

and other Haussmann streets, at whose fairy-like splendors and Aladdin-like architecture old Paris looks aghast.

Here dwell the successful speculators at the Bourse, the humbug railroad men, the hundred-and-one shrewd fellows who have made money by hanging at Louis Napoleon's heels, and receiving kicks or hints as the imperial mood dictated, and who have gathered a goodly store of treasure on occasions of hints, that when a kick came they might not be quite prostrated.

Such is a Parisian private house, — in France dignified by the name of "hôtel," while a public-house, an inn, is also a "hôtel," as with us.

This similarity of titles has led to more than one amusing mistake.

It is common with families of the old nobility (and new wealth has not yet dared to imitate this), to affix the family name over the gates of the family hôtel, there to spell out its scorn unto all plebeian passers-by, — imperial and other.

One day a newly-arrived American, on the lookout for lodgings, came across a stately house, over whose grim portals was to be seen, in time-worn letters of stone, the inscription, "HÔTEL DE LA ROCHEJAQUELIN."

"That's my style," said he;—and, beating a true republican devil-may-care tattoo with the ponderous knocker, inquired of the powdered and perfumed *laquais* what they charged for board!

Finding there was a mistake some where, he turned away with a "pshaw!" for the footman's stupidity.

By and by he met a friend, to whom he recounted what had happened.

The friend laughed, and explained the true state of the case. De La Rochejaquelin was one of the most aristocratic family names in France, and this was their city residence.

"Confound my stupidity!" said Americus.

"Go to the Hôtel du Louvre, if you want stylish board," said his friend.

"What? Oh,—ha, ha! Thank you,—no you don't! I'm not going to ask for board at Louis Nap's palace!"

The French family-circle is, of that of all

nations, the most compact, the most inseparable. Marriage dissolves no ties, but only begets new ones; and death is merely a separation for a time.

The Roman Catholic belief is beautiful for the simple, trustful faith it inspires. Souls are prayed for cheerfully and hopefully, masses sung, candles burnt: the one gone before is not a sad and vague recollection, but a vivid, ever-present spiritual reality.

The evening interior of a true French family is irresistibly quaint.

The French are fonder of innocent games than any people I know. The whole family and their visitors will play dominoes, or loto, or any of their innumerable games of chance, for hours on a stretch, with a *pari* of a few sous, — sometimes *bonbons*, — in default of these, beans.

When company is absent, and other members of the family are busy, then shall you chance to see one solitary member playing a game of "patience" by himself.

Old Frenchmen and women are often an extremely droll study, — simple, honest, and behind the age.

This type is pictured constantly on the stage, — on canvas at expositions, — in books by the best authors, — and though the subject is treated humorously, there is always a tender vein of sentiment for them displayed.

Of this class was *le capitaine Bitterlin*, a purely fictitious personage, in whose quiet adventures, as they were printed from week to week, the empress became so interested, that, after she left Paris for the sea-side, the emperor telegraphed her that Captain Bitterlin was dead.

The Captain Bitterlin was a puffy, pompous, ridiculous old fellow, — an ex-officer, whose glories lay altogether in the past; one of those funny old *militaires* who can be seen any day in a Parisian *café*, drinking sugar and water, and rattling dominoes for hours and hours together, and tending to confirm the American observer in the belief that the French have no homes.

Perhaps this poor old fellow has none; and such being the case, he might be doing a great many worse things than sitting in an open *café*, playing dominoes, and sipping orange-flower

18 *

sugar-water with a comrade, — old, pompous, and respectable, like himself.

If there be several sons in a French family, parental hearts will be sorely tried if one at least do not become a priest; and he who has taken holy orders is indeed a mother's pet.

No contact with the hateful world of money-getting for him; no marriage, with its new loves, to partly engross him, now; this dear son may be almost constantly at his mother's side, to drive with her at the Bois de Boulogne — if this be not beyond their means — to walk out with her, to shop with her, to read with her, and sit on her footstool and count the beads of his rosary while she works at home.

We can well understand the effeminate part which Monsieur l'Abbé has always played in history.

I knew a young abbé well, whose chief proficiency in life was with his needle, — the result of living almost constantly with women.

It was a strange thing to me to see him sit down with the ladies, and gravely draw out his needlework and his thimble and scissors, and go to work with the rest.

His chief passion was for worsted work; and
some of the prettiest things in his mother's drawing-room were embroidered by him. He resented
the idea of this being unmanly work.

"Other men paint on canvas with a brush,"
he said; "I paint on canvas with a needle. I
see not too much the difference."

With his long black-cloth dress, buttoned up
to the throat, and his neat low shoes and black
stockings, his beardless face, and his worsted-
work, he always seemed to me like a pure
and good woman — above the worldly vanities
and wickednesses of coquetry and dress — intent
on nothing but religion and the needle.

Every body has heard of the French *pot-au-feu.*
The making of this dish must be a national
secret.

Give an Irish cook a finer piece of beef, more
vegetables, plenty of every thing, and a cookery-
book open at the place, and she will turn you
out a potful of watery, greasy soup, and a huge
"hunk" of stringy, tough-boiled beef.

But the glories of the *pot-au-feu,* as made by
French hands, have been sung before my day.

Nothing more deliciously appetizing than that soup can ever be tasted by mortal lips; and no more succulent slice than the crisp, pinkish, boiled beef can be garnished with tomato-sauce.

I dined with the abbé's mother every Sunday for several years: she dined with me every Thursday during the same period.

Every Sunday of their lives they had the same unvarying, delicious, though plain dinner; their parents and grand-parents had so dined before them; and who can doubt that their children will follow the custom?

The dinner I commend to housekeepers. It began with the soup, — the delicious soup of the *pot-au-feu;* then came the very boiled beef which had made that soup, but which cut as firm and as tender under the mother's knife as a young turkey. Tomato-sauce with this, and boiled maccaroni in Italian style.

Then, O Nantes! one of your round, white, fat, perfumed *poulets gras!* — the roundest, tenderest, sweetest morsels that ever trod on drumsticks.

Why is it, when I see Mademoiselle Tostée,

with her plump shoulders, and white arms, I
think always of the Nantaise poulets I used to
eat at those Sunday dinners?

Salad with the poulet; dressed, — ah, I kiss
my fingers! — there are no adequate adjectives.

A tiny white cream-cheese, a cup of excellent
coffee, a thimbleful of curaçoa for the gentlemen,
if they like it, — and a delicious French dinner
— *chez soi en famille* — is over.

XV.

ABOUT ENGLISH SOCIETY IN PARIS.

HAVE often wondered that Mr. Thackeray, whom I met on many occasions in English society in Paris, should never have employed his caustic pen in delineating some of the curious phases of that society. It is not with the bold purpose of doing what Mr. Thackeray left undone that this chapter is written, but rather with the modest purpose of suggesting what he might have done with a theme so rich in the elements of pathos and humor,—at once so ludicrous and so saddening in its exhibitions.

English society in Paris is composed of two classes, which meet and mingle at parties and at balls, at church and at Galignani's reading-rooms.

The first and less important class, numerically, is made up of persons who are spoken of as " French-English ; " and among these are some of the principal editors of that Galignani's *Messenger*, newspaper, which is universally conceded to be dear in point of cost and cheap in point of political and literary importance. The French-English are not necessarily a hybrid race, though I know of many marriages between a Frenchman and an Englishwoman, and *vice versâ*, where the children, and even the parents, are classed under that head; but more frequently a French-Englishman is the son of an English father and English mother, but was born on French soil, and has lived in France all his life.

Necessarily, this person speaks French "like a native," of which fact he is rather ashamed, so proud is he of being of English parentage.

He strongly affects the society of those whom he is pleased to call his country-people, and when among the French actually attempts to speak incorrectly, so desirous is he of at once establishing what should have been his proud birthright, but

which (on account of his parents' change of residence), unhappily was not.

Apart from this foible, the French-Englishman,
for all social purposes, is far in advance of his
unalloyed "countrymen," joining to their solidity
of character a charming piquancy and attractive-
ness of conversation which is generally condemned
by the dubious qualifying word, "Frenchy."

The second class may, in contradistinction to
the first, perhaps be called the English-English,—
the English, pure and simple; that is, as pure as
men and women of high life generally are, and
as simple as rampant aristocrats must certainly
be.

These are the travelling class, "doing the continent;" the "run-over-to-Paris-for-a-day-or-two,-
just-to-cheer-you-up-a-bit,-my-boy" class; and that
other widespread class, whose members, pining
after London, still live on in Paris, and will
probably continue so to do until the debtor's
prison in England becomes, like Clichy, a thing
belonging to other and more barbarous days.

It is perhaps not very extraordinary that these
people should carefully conceal their true reason

for avoiding English soil, and ascribe their residence in Paris to many potent causes. One of the most popular of these excuses is, —

" The climate, my dear. That English climate always gives the captain the rheumatism. Ah, if it were not for the climate ! "

And the climax is a concession to French mannerisms, — the shrug.

I may use " the captain " in a general sense to represent that large class of gentlemen to whom Fleet Street invariably gives the rheumatism.

But I mind me of a particular captain, whose valorous exploits formed the subject of laughter among his acquaintances during many years in Paris, and who, no doubt fearful of rheumatism, still haunts that part of this vale of tears, the gay French capital.

The captain was a fine-looking, dashing fellow of forty or thereabouts, with a meek wife and seven children, — about the usual quota for poor Englishmen of forty. Curious to know the value of the captain's title, and with my mind somewhat confused by my American experiences of colonels, captains, generals, and the like (before the war of

19

the rebellion), I asked a titled English lady, at whose house I met him, whether he belonged to the army or the navy.

"Neither, I believe," she replied; "I think he is — ah — a sort of militia thingumy."

The gentleman was to be seen everywhere. No court ball without the captain, — no minister's fête unattended by the "militia thingumy."

Did you stroll in the direction of the great restaurants in the Palais Royal in quest of dinner, there you found the captain, who met you by twilight alone, and accosted you in a cheery voice, betokening a lightness of spirit which you would have given half your fortune to possess.

"Ah! going into the *Trois Frères* to dine?" asks the captain. And now you fancy you detect a little tremulousness in the voice.

You reply, "Yes," and of course add, "Won't you come?"

It may be the captain's acceptance is rather more enthusiastic than you expect from an Englishman, but that is no doubt the fashion of the militia thingumy.

It may be he eats his dinner with a certain eager haste, which really looks like hunger; but then are you, a mere American, a judge of the mess-room manners of English thingumy captains?

Where the captain lived was a mystery. He gave you to understand, in a general way, that it was "outside the Barrier," which afforded you wide scope for guessing, certainly, as the whole empire of France, save the capital, is outside the Barrier.

The captain also mentioned to you that you need not be at any trouble to return his calls, as he lived nearer you than you did him,—a curious computation of distances at which you smiled, but which you were willing enough to accept! He was such a jolly, splendid fellow,—so handsome, despite his iron-gray hair, so attractive, and apparently so good!

What a pity the London climate affected him so severely!

Wherever he lived, and however, the captain invariably managed to be in town for all balls, dinners, and soirées to which he had procured invitations.

Looking out of my carriage window one evening, on my way to the Tuileries, I saw the captain and his wife getting down from an omnibus at the foot of the Cours la Reine, bravely preparing to *walk* the rest of the way (they were going where I was), not even able to afford the luxury of a fiacre, obliged to take to plebeian omnibuses, and then to " Shank's mare."

Oh, unlucky rheumatism !

I am sure the captain and his wife were gayer than I was at the ball at the Tuileries.

The meek little lady was dressed in a frumpy style, which immediately stigmatized her as only another eccentric Englishwoman of wretched taste for " the toilet," by the brightly-dressed and perfumed beauties who reigned at the ball.

The captain's scarlet coat was rather faded, but that may have been the style in the British militia.

And talk of appetite at dinner ! How *did* the captain manage to dispose of so much supper at two o'clock in the morning ?

By fasting the whole day, perhaps, or the whole week, perhaps, or always.

The direful impecuniosity of this couple was one of the most painful things of my whole Paris experience, and especially saddening was their unreserved exhibition of it, — airing it at parties, dancing it at balls, and eating it ravenously at dinners.

Then, too, fresh from money-grubbing America, it struck me as strange that the captain should receive invitations to these social festivities, being, as was quite evident, altogether unable to reciprocate.

I heard the explanation one evening, coming from a host who disliked him, but who had felt himself obliged to invite him to his ball.

"A puppy, — a penniless puppy," said the old earl, "but a *gentleman*, and more's the pity!"

Another illustration of this phase of existence was furnished in the person of an English lady, the widow of a Bombay officer, who had made Paris her home for many years, though, like the captain's wife, she kept longing for England,

19 *

and within twelve hours' travel of it, never went there.

She was a "fine woman" (a recognizable term), content to know her day was over, and only · anxious to push forward and marry well her two pretty and modest daughters, who seemed to object.

She had no other title than that of simple "mistress," her husband having been "the colonel." But she had titled relations in London, of whom she was constantly talking.

"My cousin, Sir Hyppolite," she would say, " is the first barrister in England."

Another lady, and one who was received by the very first fashionable set in Paris, was also an India officer's widow, and also the mother of some handsome daughters. Unable to marry them off herself, she had confided them to a titled sister — a countess — in London, who finally accomplished the task for one of them at least, by four seasons of chaperoning at queen's levees and horticultural exhibitions.

These two widowed ladies, the cousin of Sir Hyppolite and the sister of the countess, though well acquainted with each other by name, had never met; and it happened to be my fate to perform that name-pronouncing ceremony which is an imperative preliminary to all fashionable acquaintanceship.

Mrs. Bombay, cousin to Sir Hyppolite, wished to know Mrs. Curry, sister to the countess.

I performed the name-pronouncing ceremony, and was immediately taken to task for it by Mrs. Curry.

"Not that I object to knowing Mrs. Bombay," said Mrs. Curry; "she has some decent relations; but you actually introduced *me* to her,—not her to me."

"She is much your senior," I replied. "That was sufficient cause for my action. Besides, I am an American, and do not distress myself about matters of aristocratic precedence."

"Oh, I don't mind so much for myself," answered Mrs. Curry; "but, thank goodness! my sister, the countess, did not see it."

I then went over to Mrs. Bombay.

"Handsome woman, that Mrs. Curry," said the lady. "I wanted to know her, for her family is

one of the first in England. But really, for herself personally" (a shrug) — "altogether I sha'n't
write to Sir Hyppolite that I've met her."

The great Sir Hyppolite did not seem so anxious
in regard to the welfare of Mrs. Bombay and her
daughters as they would fain have made me, as
well as the whole of English society in Paris,
believe. He occasionally sent them a letter of
introduction to some grandee who was passing
through Paris, which they did not always deliver,
fearful of an invitation to dinner not to be declined, and nothing to wear to it when received.

Once, however, the Baroness W——, an English lady who had married a Roman noble,
sent them an invitation to her ball as a sort of
response to a letter of introduction of Sir Hyppolite's, which they had delivered to her footman.

By dint of careful retrenchments at home, the
poor lady managed to get up good-enough tarle-
tans for ball-dresses for her daughters, — one can
wear tarletan to a ball, but not to a dinner, — and
I was greatly pleased by the loveliness of the
daughters in their cheap attire when I saw them
enter the ball-room.

I was standing near the baroness at the moment, and, really interested as I was in the sweetness of the girls, I was pained by her frigid reception of them. She bowed her head coldly, and bestowed upon them a blank, unmeaning stare.

"We are the cousins of Sir Hyppolite," murmured Mrs. Bombay, as if that announcement were sufficient to gain them a welcome to Paradise itself.

"Oh, yes," answered the baroness, languidly; "pray walk in the ball-room. Duke, you know that good Sir Hyppolite, don't you? These are his cousins."

The cousins bowed to the duke, who was standing next to me, and addressing me the meaningless compliments which those old beaux of the *ancien régime* are fond of paying to every young woman they meet.

The duke bowed to the Bombay ladies, and then turned to resume his conversation with me; but I advanced to the ladies, shook hands with them, and said how glad I was to see them there.

At this the duke condescended so far as

to actually address them on the subject of the weather, to their profound embarrassment.

Mrs. Bombay mustered courage to say, " Yes, my lord duke, it is very pleasant," and with this the trio subsided for the evening.

This duke was the celebrated and funny old
. Duke of B——, well known in English society for his immense and valuable diamond possessions; his curious old house in Paris, with its iron-lined walls (which he at that time erroneously supposed to be burglar-proof); his queer old carriage with its cream-colored horses; and lastly, for his elaborate but somewhat inartistic efforts for "making up" his face by means of cosmetics, which made him rather a subject for ridicule than for much respect.

On that evening he was as heavily daubed with rouge (*et noir*) as usual; and also, as usual talking of his diamonds and — his cousin; for he also had a cousin, and a cousin, too, of an importance which threw poor Sir Hyppolite quite in the shade. The cousin of the Duke of B——
was Her Britannic Majesty, Queen Victoria, and

this lady did the same cousinly duty for the duke
that Sir Hyppolite did for the Bombays.

I think the Bombays were rather "cut up"
at the cool way in which the baroness received
them.

But if they had had any of that sound practical sense which it seems to me almost impossible
to live in America without acquiring, they would
have expected nothing else. No doubt the baroness considered Sir Hyppolite quite a magnate,
but his poor relations on the continent were
another thing altogether, — as poor relations are
apt to be, even in this country.

Besides, to tell the whole truth, at the moment
they appeared she was tired of standing at the
door shaking hands with some people and curtsy-
ing to others; and furthermore, she wanted to
dance with the Duke of B——, who had asked
her, and who, while waiting, had been filling up
the time by talking diamonds to me, — one of the
subjects, by the way, on which I was and am still
shockingly uninformed.

At length the baroness was free, and the duke,
putting his arm about her substantial waist,

muttered to me, as a parting bit of wonderment,—

"I have nothing on me now that is not buttoned with a diamond."

The remark was overheard, it seems, for the *Figaro* of the following week aired the story in its columns, without contenting itself with printing the duke's initial only, as I am doing.

It was only a few weeks after this that the duke was mercilessly robbed of all his jewels by his clever but wicked groom, Henry Shaw, who, learning the secret of the iron-ribbed walls, had easily found means to accomplish his nefarious purpose.

The Bombays enjoyed themselves only moderately at the baroness' ball.

Neglected by the young men, no doubt on account of the poorness of their toilets (who says fashionable men know nothing of these things?) and overlooked altogether by the baroness after her cool reception of them, they moped about dismally, and even the supper failed to arouse them.

But Mrs. Bombay found an opportunity during the evening to communicate to me an important bit of news, —

"I think Sir Hyppolite will soon send for Helena to come stop a few weeks with him in London."

This meant a world, — that Helena, the elder daughter, was to be taken to London, and under the celestial wing of Sir Hyppolite was to soar among the loftiest of the *haute volée*, there to find a winged mate, — a baronet, or a lord, or even an earl, perhaps, — to make her his own for evermore, and invite his mother-in-law to live with them during a corresponding period.

Mrs. Bombay had but a word more with the baroness, but that word was fatal. As she and her daughters were leaving, she said, —

"*Madame la Baronne*," — for, though not one of the French-English, Mrs. Bombay had lived so long abroad that a little French would slip out occasionally, much to her annoyance, — "*Madame la Baronne*, I trust you will come to see us."

"Oh — ah — yes," replied the baroness, in a freezing tone. "What day do you receive?"

Mrs. Bombay colored a little, but like a woman of the world, had an answer ready, —

" Thursday," she replied, in a sweet tone, giving her address; and then she went her ways with her daughters.

Ah, me! If you had seen the wretched *appartement* to which the unfortunate lady with a cousin had invited this proud baroness to come, — fixing a " day of reception," at that!

A day of reception! Hollowest of mockeries! Their day of reception was every day, — their visitors their duns, and almost these alone.

For is it not clear, or have I been unconsciously veiling the melancholy fact, that Mrs. Bombay and her daughters were militia thingumies, only with a difference of sex, and that, in common with the captain, they were afflicted with that rheumatism which rendered life in London impossible, and life in Paris, or anywhere, the next thing to it?

The die was cast now. The baroness had been informed that Thursday was their reception-day, and without doubt the great lady would visit them the very next Thursday, and, in all probability, every successive Thursday, till the end of time.

Their *appartement* was on the fifth story, and was composed of three small rooms, one of which was used as a kitchen, one as a sleeping-room for the whole family; and the third and remaining one — the drawing-room, where the baroness was to be received on Thursdays — was a shabby chamber, furnished with three rickety chairs covered with faded red plush and studded with dingy brass nails, with curtainless windows, and a clock with a persistent obstinacy for half-past four.

This chamber might receive the baroness in its capacity of drawing-room, but three times a day must it return to the base uses of a dining-room, doing, as it did, a double duty. Ah, double? Triple. For at night, the weary maid-of-all-work stretched her fagged limbs on the floor, or on the centre-table, or on the chimney-piece, perhaps, for sofa or couch was there none.

Expecting the baroness' visit, on Thursday every one at the Bombays' must be up and dressed, hours, no doubt, before the baroness herself had thought of stirring.

Breakfast must not be eaten in the drawing-room on Thursday. If *Madame la Baronne* should come during its progress!

No, no. Breakfast must be eaten off the kitchen range, or in the bewilderment of the untidy little bed-room, where three people had slept, or they must go without breakfast alto-gether, rather than run the risk of having the baroness catch them at so plebeian an occupa-tion.

And to dress in order to receive the baroness!

The two girls — one sick almost unto death — vainly protested that *if* she came at all, it was scarcely probable the baroness would come so early in the morning.

If! Was there any doubt of her coming?

No. Cousins of Sir Hyppolite were not to be slighted.

All formalities had been complied with. A visiting card of "*Madame Bombay et les De-moiselles Bombay*," with their address and their

Thursday, had been left at the baroness' door within three days after her ball.

"And if" (Mrs. Bombay would observe) — " if the baroness *was* a little cool in her reception of us at her ball, — so much to think of at a ball, you know; and really, now I don't believe she quite understood, *at the moment*, that we were cousins of Sir Hyppolite."

As Thursday after Thursday passed away, and still the august baroness came not, the two girls endeavored to persuade their mother to give over these grand preparations and allow them to pursue their usual employments.

For, quite in a secret way, the elder girl turned her talent for drawing to account, and the younger wrote pretty stories in French for children, disposing of her manuscript at a beggarly price to a publisher in Lyons.

But the mother was immovable. Everything must be put aside on every Thursday, and the whole day long must the three sit with their hands folded in their laps, awaiting the visit of the baroness.

"Suppose she were to come and find you

20 *

working!" exclaimed Mrs. Bombay in answer to the remonstrance; and there was no answering that.

Three months and two additional Thursdays passed thus to my positive knowledge, and one day I saw in the London *Morning Post* that the Baroness W—— had left Paris and gone to Rome. I told Mrs. Bombay, in the hope of releasing her from her thraldom.

"Not that I care in the least for her visit," was her comment, as she tossed her head angrily; "for, after all, she is nobody. Her title was her husband's, and you know in Rome any one can buy a title for a scudo or two; and really, though I said nothing at the time, I certainly thought it odd in so old a woman as she to be dancing with that painted old fright, the Duke of B——. So, as I said, I'm quite as well satisfied that she never came on any Thursday; but really, you know, it was a shocking piece of discourtesy to my cousin, Sir Hyppolite."

Solace came, and from the source whence I, at least, was far from expecting it.

Sir Hyppolite wrote again, now extending a

positive invitation to Helena to come over an once and spend a few weeks with his family in London.

This letter caused even greater commotion than the expected visit of the baroness. The agitation of the mother and the two girls,—the desire to fit Helena out elegantly, and the lack of means to accomplish so expensive a purpose,— the struggle to be gay, with its inadequate results,—ah, it was very sad!

"You see," said the mother, "she is going into the very first society in London,—the—ve-ry— first," dropping the syllables as if they were hot, and were intended to scorch me, democratic American that I was; "and she will be under the chaperonage of *my* cousin, Sir Hyppolite."

It really seemed a pity that a pretty girl, going as her mother said, into the very first society in London from the brilliant centre of the oracles of *toilette*—Paris—should be obliged to go so poorly fitted out. But it was not to be helped.

Next came the anxiety of getting a passport, and—the passage money. But these were settled

Poor girl! Her troubles had but commenced.

The very night she arrived in London the celebrated Sir Hyppolite fell dead in a fit of apoplexy. The house where she had expected to see so much gayety was suddenly turned into a house of gloom. Her letters to her mother were a strange compound of awe, vexation, and disappointment.

Of course, the girl had no affection for this grand cousin, who had never done anything for them except serve as a medium for the mother's boasts.

Horrible as it seems to say it, there was something almost ludicrous in this sudden death, for, as Mrs. Bombay remarked, "It seemed done on purpose to spite her." And whether her tears were tears of annoyance or tears of grief, it was not easy to determine.

Helena returned to Paris in little more than a week after she had left it.

The other lady, Mrs. Curry, was more fortunate. She had a very small but fixed income, and her daughter, by her beauty and grace, was youth of London. No doubt she would soon be married off; and there was another to follow her footsteps and be married off in turn.

But the marrying-off took four long and dissipated seasons to accomplish, and during the accomplishment the beautiful girl came over to see her mother in Paris.

Her boxes, her flounces, her jewels, and herself (worst and most unmanageable of all) were to be crowded into the little *appartement* where her mother worried and fretted the year through. The visits seemed to afford little comfort to either party.

"A *piggish* place you live in, mamma! A a hole, — a wretched little entre*sole*" (drawling out the last syllable in that manner so repulsive to the French ear). "What *do* you do it for?"

"My child, you are spoiled," returns the mother, gravely. "R
not an ea

But these Paris visits to mamma in the wee little entre*sole* are few, far between, and of short duration. Miss Curry soon returns to London, and chaperoned by her aunt, the countess, her name appears again almost daily in the columns of the *Morning Post*, as having graced the queen's drawing-room with her presence, or inhaled the perfume of a rare rose at the last horticultural show with her aristocratic and well-cut little nose.

Here I take occasion to say that what I have written is true in every particular.

It must not be supposed that the captain of the militia thingumy, the Bombays, and the Currys, if real people at all, were poor wretches striving to obtain a foothold in society, failing in it and being properly snubbed by all people with any pretentions to good breeding.

I have, of course, given fictitious names to these people, but to their friends I need not.

At the house of Mrs. Curry, His Royal Highness the Duke of Cambridge was a visitor; as also the Duke and Duchess of Hamilton (Princess

of Baden), with their son, the Marquis of
Douglas, the Earl and Countess of Fife, and
the Earl and Countess of Kinnoul.

These people, very elegant and distinguished,
and possessors of immense estates (Lord and Lady
Fife are close neighbors of the Queen in Scot-
land, and are favorites with Her Majesty, who
frequently visits them), are of course real personages of birth and lineage.

Sir Hyppolite (with another name) *was a* magnate in London. His sudden death was deplored
by all.

And even the captain, the militia thingumy,
was acknowledged to be a "gentleman," even by
the proud old earl who called him a "penniless
puppy."

Therefore these people can not properly be
classed among snobs.

A snob is a
ners of h

was the only claim to distinction of the █ which I have presented types.

Pride of money is better than this. Money made will sometimes bear testimony to talent, — almost always to tact or ingenuity; while this absurd and shabby pride of birth is proof of neither tact, talent, ingenuity, nor industry.

THE END.

www.ingramcontent.com/pod-product-compliance
Lightning Source LLC
Chambersburg PA
CBHW020107030726
47498CB00006B/1994